DAUGHTERS OF AN AMBER NOON

KATHERINE V. FORREST

DAUGHTERS OF AN AMBER NOON

alyson books
los angeles | new york

All characters in this book are fictitious. Any resemblance to real individuals—either living or dead—is strictly coincidental.

Manufactured in the United States of America.

This trade paperback original is published by Alyson Publications,
P.O. Box 4371, Los Angeles, California 90078-4371.
Distribution in the United Kingdom by Turnaround Publisher Services Ltd.,
Unit 3, Olympia Trading Estate, Coburg Road, Wood Green,
London N22 6TZ England.

First edition: September 2002

02 03 04 05 06 a 10 9 8 7 6 5 4 3 2 1

ISBN 1-55583-663-1

Library of Congress Cataloging-in-Publication Data
Forrest, Katherine V., 1939–
Daughters of an amber noon / Katherine V. Forrest.—1st ed.
Sequel to: Daughters of a coral dawn.
ISBN 1-55583-663-1
1. Lesbians—Fiction. I. Title.
PS3556.O737 D33 2002
813'.54—dc21 2002071669

Credits

- Excerpt from *Three Guineas* by Virginia Woolf, © 1938 by Harcourt Inc. and renewed 1966 by Leonard Woolf, reprinted by permission of the publisher.
- Cover photography by Photodisc.
- Cover design by Matt Sams.

To Jo Hercus

for all the new worlds

As a woman I have no country. As a woman I want no country. As a woman my country is the whole world.

—Virginia Woolf

2199.8.30—OLYMPIA

It has been the eternity of twenty-four hours since the penultimate day in the existence of our Unity.

One day ago we bade farewell to the four thousand one hundred and forty-four of us who have departed on a great adventure: to find a permanent new home in space, hidden, beyond encroachment by Earth.

Yesterday: a time of rejoicing, of celebration, exhilaration.

Today: a desolation of bereavement that spares not one of the two thousand and fifty-one of us who remain here, root-bound on our turbulent and noxious home planet.

With my beloved sister Minerva off to the stars as eyewitness-recorder of their divergent chapter in the history of our Unity, I, Olympia, find myself called upon to replace her—as if anyone could replace Minerva, the historian. Still, I must attempt to assume her responsibilities, even though my efforts will be but a pallid emulation of her brilliance and distinction.

From this day forward, I am no longer Olympia the philosopher. I am Olympia the historian, recorder of the continuing history of our Sisterhood on Earth.

2199.9.30—OLYMPIA

Our Unity is again gathered in the inland desert of Southern Calivada, in the location where we first met more than seven months ago. We occupy the same refuge Kendra dropped into place back then, an inflated camouflage dome that from the air resembles ancient, blackened bomb craters—the purpose to which this brutalized land was put in centuries past. Our dome provides a cloak of invisibility, Rakel taking the additional and very necessary precaution of spraying its ceiling to deflect body heat–seeking sensors. Over the past month we have arrived at this place from different directions and by using individual flight paks, knowing that traveling here by any other conveyance or in groups would trigger satellite surveillance.

Seven months ago, when we reached the shattering decision that a majority of us would seek a new home in the stars, our entire Unity focused its energies on facilitating their escape. The perils they face as they now navigate their way through the solar system to the Einsteinian Curve, pursued by Earth's military might, defy my powers of imagination. But their escape is thus far successful: a fact confirmed through our own information-monitoring sources and by public conjecture and rumors, rumors vehemently denied by officials who also deny the existence of such a flight. We draw considerable comfort from this. If our sisters' ship were captured or destroyed, there would be immediate disclosure and Earth's military would be gloating.

Although we have our reasons for remaining on Earth, we are no less in exile from our home planet than those en route to the stars. Under no circumstances will we continue to contribute our intellectual gifts to Earth's leadership as it is presently constituted. We fully concede that all our efforts—our infiltration of the halls of power over five generations, our labor, our gifts of persuasion—have come to naught. None of it has changed or deflected this planet's predication of supremacy on armament and conflict and subjugation. We will not corrupt ourselves by using any of their weaponry or any we could create to fight them; our Unity rejects, reviles, repudiates the use of violence and weapons of destruction to attain and hold power.

Our Mother, whose diminutive body is our origin, whose all-encompassing mind and gargantuan spirit are the fountainhead of our existence, spoke to us from this very stage, and the image of her—resplendent in her green lustervel robe, arms crossed as she addressed the six thousand of us—is indelible, as are her words: "It has never been the female nature to seek or want power." As Mother so witheringly pointed out, "In this primitive culture we have been at the whim of its inferior leadership." Then she put forth her ultimate recommendation in her pithy, inimitable way: "My dear ones, let's just get the hell out of here."

And we have.

Although we worked mostly behind the scenes in the world we abandoned, by any definition we held a considerable measure of influence. We occupied vital positions in all the professions key to the successful conduct of Earth's progress: the sciences, commerce, politics, spirituality, all cultural interchange. Thus, we phased out our withdrawal cautiously, unobtrusively, like stars in a canopy blinking out one by one.

Our collective absence has been calamitous. Our previous influence in tempering international hostilities and economic tyranny is more than painfully obvious in the two-week-old military takeover by Theo Zedera, the loathsome and universally feared Premier Supreme whom everyone refers to with the appropriately ugly name Zed. With living conditions plummeting to deplorable depths, he continues to consolidate his power by obliterating all opposition, his troops brutally mopping up any vestige of resistance. Guerrilla warfare has all but ceased, and even the historically contentious renegade Eastern and Arab blocs have capitulated. Just when it appeared that humankind had managed to advance to the point of shedding itself of megalomaniac rulers, Zed has seized the invincible power that Napoleon, Hitler, Stalin, and Zhou only dreamed of—the key difference in his strategy being that he represents no nation, only his grandiose view of his own new world order.

Amid this triumphal takeover we, however, are the discordant note. The lone remaining symbol of defiance. The consternation at our disappearance, the impotent fury at the audacity and success of our escape, can be inferred from the gearing up of the search. Zed's henchmen have begun to scour the planet for any lead to us, any trace. Careful not to disseminate the truth—the full scope of our disappearance—Zed's central news dispensary has reported as missing several dozen of the most famous among us, including Africa and Tara and Viridia, and has offered vast rewards for information leading to their discovery. If they do manage to intercept our sisters as they venture into the stars, or if they capture any of us who remain earthbound, death will be infinitely preferable to what would follow—and of course death would be a component of the incarceration, degradation and slavery that would follow.

Where will we go, how will we live? How do we continue to conceal ourselves from our lethal enemies and their resources? How do we redirect our considerable energies and all our talents into a drastic transformation of our lives?

As Mother made her way to the service ship for transit to the starship *Amelia Earhart* one month ago, leaving us to conduct our lives and our future on this ravaged planet, she smiled and issued the same vote of confidence she has given us all our lives: "I'm sure you girls can manage."

She had no concept of Theo Zedera.

2199.10.06—OLYMPIA

We have spent these past six days in our desert compound absorbed in discussion and information analysis, forming and reforming into enclaves, our meetings extending late into each night. Six months ago, Tara made a viable and altogether ingenious proposal for a future habitat that was greeted at that time with skepticism and resistance. But that was before Zed. We pore over its possibilities now, assessing the most complex questions of geology, agriculture and horticulture, psychology, hydrology, atmospherics, structural design, volcanology. There is no hint of rancor in any of the discussions, only a searching evaluation of our challenges, a weighing of all possible answers.

Anguished over our vanished sisters, consumed by planning and decision-making, we work tirelessly, unmoved by brilliant, crystalline desert nights. Sexuality has dimmed among us, the blazing carpet of stars flung across skies of ebony velvet having little allure; it is simply a vast cold entity that has swallowed up our sisters...

I, Olympia the historian, and my sister, Isis the mathematician, especially feel the urgency of our situation. We are the only members of Mother's Inner Circle—daughters born directly to her—who have chosen to remain on Earth. Of our original nine, from whom all the generations of our Unity have descended, beloved Selene long ago perished in a deep-sea diving accident off Antarctica; and Demeter, Diana, Hera, Minerva, Venus and Vesta have accompanied Mother into space. I feel my separation from them with knifelike keenness.

For this night of decision we have exercised, as the elders of our Unity, the prerogative of choosing the presenter to summarize the choices we have made, and those still to be determined. Young as she is, Tara is the logical choice on all counts. Isis and I wish to acknowledge her for the ingenuity of her proposal, and to evaluate her leadership potential at this perilous time—to observe her conduct among a divergent group ranging in age from twenty-five years her junior to more than eighty years her senior. We call ourselves a Unity, but we are a tumult of nonconformist, independent, confident, indeed arrogant women—women who nonetheless require leadership, as Mother well knew; but anyone attempting to don that mantle must run a daunting gauntlet, as Megan learned when Mother anointed her to lead the expedition to the stars. But leadership we must have, be that one leader or several. We require the coordination of all our talents.

The Unity has assembled in a semicircle of tiers rising above a central platform where Isis and I now enter in our amber ceremonial robes. Tara is already there and stands slightly behind where we sit, her arms crossed, gazing at the colorful, noisy, unruly array. Amid women clad in a rainbow assortment of pants and shirts and trouser suits, she is the color of sun and sand with her pale hair, dune-colored pants and shirt, and dusty desert boots. The youngest of Regina's three daughters, Tara ranks with the most brilliant scholars ever to walk the corridors of Oxford. Her restless energy, that impatient intelligence in her gray eyes, are vibrant echoes of Megan, her extraordinary sister.

At my signal she takes one stride forward, arms at her side, her tall body straight and tense. "My sisters," she begins, her resonant, unamplified voice filling the dome, vastly different from the bell-like tones of her sister's voice but no less commanding: silence and stillness descend. "Esteemed Olympia, esteemed Isis," she says, turning slightly toward us, "I am honored to share this platform with you." Isis and I nod, pleased by her graciousness.

Tara addresses the Unity gravely, formally. "As we all know, since our withdrawal the search for us has become relentless. We dare not risk the slightest exposure, we dare not be careless—our enemies have surely determined that not all of us escaped into space on the *Amelia Earhart*." I see a shadow deepening the gray of her eyes, and it occurs to me to wonder what possible reason would compel this young woman to remain here. But then, each member of our Unity has her own reasons for her decision.

Tara continues: "The first consensus we arrived at is that we will remain together."

Even though this conclusion has been apparent for days, an approving murmur rises from most of our Unity. Most, but not all. I myself am pleased that additional painful separation will not be added to what we have already suffered.

"Our great challenge," Tara says somberly, "is to reinforce the safety of ourselves and our children by remaining invisible. We have therefore chosen one of the most formidable and forbidding areas of our Earth. And now, my sisters, we will review the strategy to make this place on our Mother Earth into our new home."

2199.11.15

General Lucan Desmond strode down a long, sculpture-lined corridor in the Premier's current residence, a sun-splashed palatial compound overlooking the pellucid waters of Montego Bay, Jamaica.

Smoothing the jacket of a black-and-gold dress uniform that did not need smoothing, Desmond returned the simultaneous salute of four stone-faced, black-clad sentries standing at attention beside the Premier's office suite. He then passed under the DNA scanner, pricklingly aware that a negative reading would result in his cremation by laser beams. The two-second probe culminated in the automatic opening of the door to the Premier's office. Desmond marched a dozen steps in precise cadence across the antique oriental carpet, saluted, and stood at attention.

Premier Supreme Theo Zedera, as usual, was in the company of Esten Balin, who was hunched over an array of monitors in a corner alcove and did not acknowledge Desmond, did not so much as move his bulk or raise his bald head from his work. The room was scented with the faintly sweet aroma of Balin's stim-soaked cigar.

The Premier sat behind an onyx desk, his chair framed by a huge bay window open to a vista of palms and ferns against an azure sky. Chunkily muscular in a close-fitting gray silk tunic, he had also not looked up at Desmond's entrance; he was absorbed in a dark-hued portrait of a diaphanous woman on the wall to his left, a painting that Desmond had heard dated from the nineteenth century. Smiling faintly, the Premier moved the fingers of one hand to the strains of a violin concerto bathing the room.

Desmond took the opportunity to stare at him, once more attempting to take some measure of this man as a man, not a dictator. The Premier was, in truth, handsome, a fact obscured by a reputation that branded him as fearsome, pitiless, subhuman. In profile his large head appeared sculpted, his hair dark and thick, his florid features Romanesque; his eyes were thickly lashed and his full lips were faintly curved in a sensual smile.

At the close of a musical phrase, the Premier touched a panel on his desk, and turned his leonine head to stare at Desmond, the music cut off, the smile gone.

Desmond held the dark, lengthy gaze with difficulty, yet with a degree of equanimity as well. He knew of no one who was not thoroughly intimidated by the combination of searing intelligence and implacable ruthlessness in this man who had unflinchingly ordered the incineration of cities and nations.

The Premier finally spoke in a husky, soft voice. "Sit down, General."

As Desmond lowered himself into a brocade-covered armchair, the Premier lifted a velvet-shod foot to rest it on the corner of his desk and steepled his fingers. "Where are they?"

Desmond forced his body into a semblance of relaxation. He cleared his throat. "We have considerable information and many leads, sir. We're following them up thoroughly."

"Meaning you still have no idea where they are."

"We're closing in on them; we're absolutely confident we'll capture them."

"Yes." The Premier eased his foot off the desk and leaned forward, hands flat on the desk, fingers splayed. "Just as you were absolutely confident you'd capture their escape vessel. Right up to the moment they vanished into space and laughed in our faces while they did it."

To be out-thought and outsmarted by *women*... Heat suffused Desmond, intensified by the expression on the Premier's face: amused contempt.

Desmond ground out his reply: "A miscalculation that won't happen again, I guarantee it. We've kept a tight lid on news of the escape."

"Rumors have escaped your so-called tight lid."

Desmond shrugged. "They always do, sir. But they're just rumors. Anyone involved knows how they'll die if they so much as hint they know anything." Balin would get them. He could feel Balin's malevolence permeating the room. He was always aware of Esten Balin. "We'll find that ship—we're using full telescopic overlap trace scans."

"Overlap scans in open space," the Premier ruminated, half-smiling. He picked up a malachite pen. "Locating their ship will be as easy as locating a needle in the Sahara."

"Sir," Desmond said doggedly, "you're right that it may take some luck to locate them in space, but we have another solution. You do agree with our assessment that not all escapees left on that ship?"

"An obvious hypothesis." The Premier fingered the iridescent green pen. "Which took a week to arrive at when Africa Contrera could have given me the same answer in half an hour with half the evidence."

"Sir, there's never been anyone like Africa Contrera," Desmond protested.

"No."

The Premier had spoken the word with an emotion Desmond could not identify, and Desmond, remembering the Premier's previous closeness to her, said, "She's a genius."

"A genius who's taken her genius with her." Desmond flinched at the harshness of his tone. "Along with the genius of everyone else who left with her. Somehow no one in my Secret Service managed to notice that women in key positions were vanishing one by one."

The Premier waved away Desmond's attempt at a reply. "From your report of the schematics of that ship and the equipment they bought on the black market, I understand it's outfitted to hold forty-two hundred at the very outside."

"Correct, sir. Meaning that the rest of them are still here. Including perhaps Africa Contrera—"

"Yes."

"And when we find them—"

"We'll gain information to lead us to the others—a more useful and reliable tool than space scans. You have no limitations whatsoever on the manpower and equipment at your disposal, Desmond. Find them."

"Yes, sir." And with barely concealed eagerness Desmond asked, "Any restrictions?"

"Certainly," the Premier said with irritation. "Do whatever is necessary to anyone you think has information, but I want any woman you find brought to me alive. Tell your men the capture of any of them wins a bonus of ten years' privileges. Provided the women are delivered unharmed. Completely unharmed. Am I clear on this?"

"Absolutely clear, sir." Ten years' privileges was an enormous bonus, but Desmond had hoped to make freedom to use the women an additional inducement to his troops. After all, it had been the Premier's order to enhance their testosterone levels, and sexual aggressiveness required slaking along with the stoking. But Desmond had learned that none of the Premier's orders were issued by whim; there was rationale behind everything. Still, he might rescind this particular restriction when Esten Balin, with his infinite gifts for such work, thoroughly and excruciatingly extracted information from the first few women to be brought to the Premier...

The Premier said in dismissal, "I want you and your aides in the council chamber tomorrow at nine o'clock for a full strategy review."

"Yes, sir."

As Desmond rose from his chair, the Premier again placed a foot on the corner of his desk, then said in an easy, almost jovial tone, "This is the last piece in what we need to accomplish, Desmond. Find these women and I'll see to it that you're a very happy man for the rest of your days. If not..."

Desmond saluted. "I guarantee results, Premier."

With limitless manpower and technology at his disposal, he felt all the confidence he had expressed; yet, as he marched from the office, he could not help stealing a glance at Esten Balin.

Balin had lifted his gaze from his monitors. His thin lips, clamped around his cigar, were curved into an arctic, predatory smile.

2199.12.10—JOSS

When I say I'm putting on the theatrical performance of the century...well, the century comes to a close in a few weeks, so what does that say? To be in an all-female world every day, without pretense or secrecy, without having to bear all the male assumptions—it's miraculous. Especially when I have unsisterly feelings toward one of my sisters. Not that she knows it. Not that anyone knows it, or has ever known it. Or even suspects that she's the sole reason I chose to stay here.

Fainthearted me. From age two, when I first learned to read, history told me that this world I found so visually beautiful and spiritually wondrous, an inspiration for my very early creation of music, is in reality a place of terror. When I look at human history, what stands out? Atrocities. Bloody conquests since time began. Leaders of conscripted armies standing on mounds of corpses and thumping their chests in glory. I've learned that history has its own parallels to geological epochs, one era of shattering horror after another, with civilization in between times muddling back to some degree of evolvement and a revival of naïve hope that things would remain that way. After the biological attacks between India and China and those inconceivable one hundred and seventy million deaths from hemorrhage, it seemed only nuclear annihilation of the planet was left to be perpetrated by humankind. Again we've made the mistake of underestimation. Apparently nuclear destruction would be too cleansing and final for the human species. Since our Sisterhood abandoned the outside world, what's happened out there is well beyond my powers of comprehension.

Even so...even so, how long can I stand how we live now? This is too different. Far too strange.

During the meetings under the camouflage dome, I sided with the faction contending that our Unity form smaller groups and fan out into all the deserts. "I not only know what living on the surface would mean in terms of technology, I embrace that knowledge," I argued to my sisters. "All of us admire the fiercely independent nomadic tribes who've held so closely to their heritage and customs over the centuries that they shunned the presence of an entire realm of technology in their lives and homelands. We couldn't have any of our 'bots or synthesizers or garbtechs, no hologames, nothing. These would be visible anomalies in desert areas, too easy for sensors to pick up for a trace. Can we not accept that?"

"We'd have to live too much like the ancients," Makana countered. "Our lives would be a struggle to achieve minimal living conditions. Even if we succeeded, did everything right to conceal ourselves, they could still pick up DNA and pinpoint us to an area—and do this from the faintest trace, from anything our skin touched..."

Then Africa spoke, wonderful Africa. Quietly, as she always does. "There's no underestimating the lengths they'll go to find us, Joss. So we'd need to endure skin coating on top of our other discomforts."

Ugh. What was I to say to that?

My allies, my comrades continued the argument for

me. Daria, small in stature and wiry, intensity gathered in her dark eyes, offered the most compelling summary and imagery: "Small bands of us would be safe in the severely hostile deserts. In South America, in the Patagonia—the coldest desert in the world. Or the Atacama, the driest—though it's heavily contaminated with boron. The Sahara and the Gobi—we'd have the advantage of their huge land mass. The Namib—we'd have cover under its pervasive fogs. Rub al Khali—its murderous quicksands. The major dune area in Australia's Simpson Desert is difficult terrain even for its indigenous people."

Hope rose in me when I heard Isis murmur, "I love Australia...Estrella came from Australia...." And Olympia added dreamily, "As did my Celestc, who was born in Perth..."

I took advantage of these overheard comments to quickly suggest, "We could blend in with the nomadic people who still live in the Simpson Desert. Who live in all deserts except this one." The reason this one is uninhabited did not need to be stated: It is lethally poisoned. I argued, "We wouldn't be permanently separated—small units of each group would be able to visit unobtrusively with other groups...b"

Then Isis spoke. Her statement was made quietly, but it might as well have been thundered: "If any one of us were captured, she could bring disaster to us all."

In the brief, decisive discussion that followed, my sisters skirted any specifics of what being captured would entail. Meaning that the worst horrors I can imagine probably aren't horrible enough. "Look," I desperately offered, "those who choose to live above ground could have a poison pill, a toxin hidden in a tooth that we'd release by uttering a specific combination of guttural sounds—I read about it one time in one of those historical spy novels," I concluded lamely.

Isis kindly, gently pointed out, "Our enemies would paralyze us, scan us, then simply extract the poison."

"Still," I grumbled, "there must be a foolproof way we could destroy ourselves if need be."

But she had won the day.

I have to concede that at least we're safe here, as safe as we can be, and the two-edged sword of technology is making all of this happen. Every hour of the day and night our 'bots bore into rock, coating everything with Opaquit and Fluxbar. If invaders come, their on-the-scene probes would expose the cavities where we excavate, but the ones from satellite scans can't sense anything except the igneous and metamorphic rock that's supposed to be here.

Living in this place means we can bring all our technology with us. Our tech-nerds may be the happiest among us—they continue their careers of research and development. Lucky them.

I sound more ungrateful than I am. I've seen the design for our community, and it's as creative and intricate as anyone would expect from the talent of our Sisterhood. The quarters I share with a half dozen sisters my age is a prototype and we love it. It's ours to evaluate and suggest improvements. The rest of my sisters, with the exception of esteemed Isis and Olympia, live communally in large chambers because of the necessary priorities of focusing on the basics of food, water, and concealment. Eventually we will expand enough to allow anyone who wishes solitude to have her own quarters. I will be one of those because the idea of sharing my quarters with the one I love has never even approached the realm of fantasy; she could not be more remote if she were a constellation where my sisters now venture. I wish to be by myself, and during those hours when my labors are not required in the building of our world here, I will work on my music.

In these chambers, along with the usual necessities of daily living are many objects not only of beauty but of consolation. Veined multicolored rock samples that sculptor Makana has fashioned into sensuous art for us. A very few precious mementos we brought with us from our former lives. Several walls are hung with holoscenes, audible if we choose them to be: leafy trees blowing in a gusting wind; rain or snow falling; the night skies; and my favorite, what I miss most, ocean waves. Another wall, curved like the distant horizon, slowly mutates through deepening hues into sunset, an endless series of them.

Paradoxically, for all my resistance to being here, the walls I have grown to love hold projected images from the valley we occupy, a land majestic in its terrible grandeur. These images come from recorders so minute and low-powered that they could be grains of sand on the desert landscape, undetectable. I've been watching a storm come in over the mountains, which we have just renamed the Lyon-Martins. These mountains, upthrust breasts from Mother Earth, are nobly ancient and seamed with folds, as rich with warm toned color as old bones, beige melding through every autumn shade of brown and gold, with patches of speckled green from croppings of trees, some yellow patches of flowers. I've watched towers and layers of gray dimming the mountains into indistinctness, the folds of land darkening in the foothills. Away from the mountains the sky is lightening, clouds of stone gray.

Another wall shows the valley floor, rock nettle, salt bush, creosote, cottonwood and mesquite trees, and sometimes the brave occupants of this valley, ravens and turkey vultures, pack rats, kit fox, coyotes, who emerge when this furnace-hot land begins its evening cooling. And of course those desert fixtures, snakes and lizards in all their infinite variety and unsettling beauty.

Yesterday we had a sandstorm, preceded by a number of willy willies, those slender desert whirlwinds that pirouette madly over the landscape in a silly twist of wind and sand. I've learned that in a sandstorm the land acquires a pinkish-tan color and patterns of sand wash over the landscape.

Approaching rain darkens the landscape to tan, and colors in the rock emerge, the land turning reddish, pinkish, brick-tan, then brackish, finally dissolving in a murkiness of mist. The mountains become invisible, the hills indistinct, homogenous in the distance, with only a few dark green spots of foliage. The sky lightens almost to white as rain settles in, the colors on the land variegated tans with an overlay of green foliage. I could spend hours in these chambers—and I do. Except there is one overriding awareness.

The air smells odd. Same thing in all the other finished areas—the air smells different. Olympia claims this is impossible; it's perfectly constituted oxygen matched to the Earth's atmosphere. But I smell what I smell, and some of my sisters agree with me. I can't get away from it unless I breathe into cloth. It's everywhere.

I miss outside. Rain. Ocean. Flowers. Birds. Cities and culture and history, no matter how terrible. I long for the sun on my face, even the murderous sun of this desert. Warming my shoulders, my back. My thighs.

Why in the world did I stay here? How could I have been stupid enough to stay because of a woman I can only know from afar?

2200.1.01—OLYMPIA

It is very early in the morning on this day that launches us into a new century. In my role of historian, I dutifully accompany Tara and a precocious young descendant of mine, Joss, for a first look at Bannon Crater, and I also take my first trip along the newly opened major passageway that we have named DeBeauvoir Corridor. We travel in what someone has whimsically but aptly dubbed a gopher cart, a tiny, hydrogen-powered, very basic and most exquisitely uncomfortable vehicle, especially when piloted by Tara, whose priority is plainly efficiency of movement. Thanks to the bouncing, swerving ride, I am able to note scarcely anything other than a blur of brilliantly lighted igneous rock walls.

"Ours, esteemed Olympia. Every inch of these walls—ours," Joss exults as we careen along. "We've decided to cover them in murals."

So the younger members of our Unity will decorate this vast corridor as they choose. An ingenious assignment considering our living circumstances, even if it is nowhere close to a solution to the problems we face with some of our youngest women who chose to remain on Earth but never imagined they would end up here. Still, the results should be colorful and unique. Not so colorful or unique, I trust, that a blindfold will be necessary for my equilibrium on my next trip, assuming I survive this one.

Dear Joss, her arm around my shoulders, holds me securely until the gopher cart slows and stops. I emerge unscathed and with most of my dignity intact. We approach the view panels overlooking Bannon Crater...

This time Joss clutches me for support. "Great Geezerak," she squawks.

I am pleased, not only because this twenty-year-old has chosen a favored phrase of Mother's but that she has spoken first, saving posterity from whatever inanity would have issued from my own mouth at the astonishing spectacle before us.

Hearing a soft chuckle, I manage to wrench my gaze away to see Tara, hands bracing her narrow hips, observing us with a wide grin; then she quickly strides away to immerse herself in the array of harmonic charts she has come here to monitor. Joss too is looking at Tara. With her solid and strong body, her dark hair and blue eyes, Joss is a handsome contrast to blade-slim, blond, gray-eyed Tara. The matchmaker in me wonders if the youngster is taken with her. A good many women stand in that particular line. The role of leadership, which Tara fills with consummate grace, has heightened her magnetism.

I return to the view panels, and Joss and I stare down into a boiling caldera separated from us by this thinnest of barriers whose strength I trust on the shakiest of faith.

I know Bannon Crater is a half-mile across and more than seven hundred feet deep, but I can see neither across it nor into its ultimate depths. What I do see are coal-black and deeply reddish crater walls glowing in fiery reflection of red-gold molten juvenile lava moving sluggishly toward a declivity on the far side of the crater. Steam rises high into the atmosphere, a purple-gray vision I could not conjure in a nightmare, giant clouds irradiated by a faint preternatural brightening suggesting sunrise—hallucinatory, a Dante's inferno.

I have to remind myself that the caldera is central to the success of our Unity's defenses against discovery.

Tara, Joss, and I stand on a rough rock observation platform at the end of this underground corridor excavated to the edge of a volcano that last erupted about six thousand years ago. Cursory research—well, all right, I asked Viridia—has told me this volcano is classified as a maar, a void in the earth caused by collapse after a violent expulsion of magma. It's a miniscule version of the enormous crater in the Pacific Northwest forming Yellowstone Park, which is also a maar; that one was created two million years ago by a explosion so cataclysmic that its nuclear winter–like dust cloud extinguished much of the life existing on the planet at that time.

Previous maps identify our crater as Ubehebe Crater—before we renamed it in honor of a twentieth-century trailblazer, as we have renamed all of the places in this valley. Ten thousand or so years ago, the area where we stand was covered by an immense Pleistocene lake hundreds of feet deep, created by the melting of glaciers during the great Ice Age. The lake gradually dried out during the Holocene, forming a vast salt pan far below sea level, two hundred and twenty-eight feet at its lowest point—unique on the North American continent. This depth of land resulted in summer heat so intense it killed some of its first explorers, resulting in the appropriate, if dramatic, appellation of Death Valley. The name turned out to be far more appropriate and dramatic—and prophetic—than anyone living at that time could have imagined.

"Unbelievable," Joss breathes.

Tara moves toward us. "Do you know the history of this area, Joss?"

Of course she does. Joss has studied history extensively. Her hands stuffed deep in her pants pockets, she answers shyly, modestly, "I know it used to be a twentieth-century military test site. Top secret experiments, nuclear and biological weapons. Then they turned it into a nuclear and biological waste dump." Her sapphire eyes narrow. "And that laid the foundation for calamity."

Tara nods, and I confirm sorrowfully, "That's correct, Joss. They couldn't have laid the groundwork for ecological calamity any better had they set out intentionally to do it."

A twenty-first century United States Congress, with hubris reminiscent of the planners of the *Titanic*, compounded all previous felonies perpetrated on this cruelly tortured land by accepting manufacturers' claims about so-called impenetrable containers; they approved burial of nuclear waste and other toxins in what was then Nevada.

"The earthquakes." Joss has made all the historical connections. "That was the end of all human habitation here."

I shake my head as I remember the history too, the four great San Andreas Fault earthquakes and endless aftershocks from 2051 to 2063 and the concomitant volcanic activity that not only ruptured what was the northern coast of California but acted as a leviathan blending machine in Nevada. Magma broke through the upper mantle of the earth, and before it receded the edge of a flow dissolved the so-called impenetrable containers of nuclear waste and caused their dispersal throughout the West Coast's major aquifer like poison injected into Mother Earth's veins. The contamination spread underground to man-made Lake Meade, near a famously garish place called Las Vegas. This pleasure mecca, battered by earthquake damage, then bereft of potable water, became a sand-blown ghost town virtually overnight. Of course, a facsimile, the pleasure capital we know as Vega, reappeared with record speed in the

Midwest. So transmogrified was the California-Nevada landscape that it became known as Calivada. And as for this place...

"Death Valley," Joss says. "In every sense of the name."

At the forlorn look on Joss's face I smile and say brightly, "It's ours now, and it's Sappho Valley." I am very well aware that Joss is among the young women conflicted about being here. "Lethally contaminated as it is, we have reclaimed it, we have made it ours, we will renew it." Surely in ways no one could expect.

"It was a brilliant idea of yours," Joss says to Tara in a mixed tone that concedes admiration.

"Only the concept, and a vague one at that," Tara demurs. "The entire Sisterhood further explored and contributed research and plans. We were lucky to have Viridia."

"Your concept was much more than vague," I tell Tara, who thanks me with a grin. But she is right about Viridia. Her brilliance in the field of macrogeology, luckily for us, includes a specialty in volcanology.

Joss says softly, "I still think we could have done this in other places." The bruised look in her eyes disturbs me.

"Perhaps," Tara answers simply. Then adds, "But this place offers a singular advantage: Bannon Crater. And fear of volcanoes is primal, Joss. It's never occurred to anyone—even the power-mad who care nothing about what they may destroy—to duplicate a volcano except for the hologram lab models like those Viridia used to test out our theories."

I gaze at the dramatics outside our window, thinking of how volcanoes are so indispensable a factor in the formation of land mass and the shaping of land, yet an omnipotent scourge in their unpredictable destructiveness—attested to by many buried civilizations, ancient and modern. We've taken full advantage of this legendary history of disaster.

This volcano is our own. It is not Mother Earth but we ourselves who have brought Bannon Crater to life. The volcano, though its caldera heaves awesomely with lava and issues clouds of steam into the stratosphere, remains technically extinct. The effects of its exudations on the atmosphere and environment are, if anything, beneficial.

We chose this radical solution because of two intractable problems. First, to remain invisible from the heat-sensing, acutely detailed observations of orbital probes, and second, to elude the systematic hunt conducted by crack ground troops with the most sophisticated tracking equipment—all of it under the command of the formidable Zed and his henchmen. To contend with these threats, we have risked playing with Earth's primal fire.

Because the foreseeable future holds little hope that our present home will be temporary, we have another problem, in its own way equally daunting: to contend with the displacement felt by members of our Unity—like young Joss. Like myself, for that matter...I could not leave with my sisters because my roots are too bound into this Earth for me to countenance living on an alien landscape. We have suffered a massive dislocation, however, and much as we savor being together, we spend hours with our psychologists mourning the loss of our former lives, our longing to reclaim something of them...

"How did we manage to do this? I fully understand the theory but only some of the logistics," Joss says, gesturing at the crater.

The technicalities of bringing a dormant volcano to life are well beyond the ken of a mere philosopher-historian like myself. I trust that Tara will give Joss an account that will be accessible to me as well.

Tara rests her elbows on a chest-high railing fronting the observation window. "It began two and a half months ago. Rakel and her team donned protective cloaks, and over a period of days and under cover of several convenient sandstorms, they sank small-diameter bores far into the earth around Bannon Crater, dispersing debris from these bores into the caldera. Then they tamped small delay-fusion charges deep into these bores. We've been detonating them in a carefully controlled erratic sequence, producing harmonic tremors and earthquake-swarm readings on seismic scales all over the world—these shallow earthquakes suggesting not tectonic faulting, but magma moving closer to the surface, classic evidence of burgeoning volcanic activity. Then, our fusion fuses ignited treated rocks in the caldera and liquefied them into a lava flow."

"Dangerous," Joss commented, peering into the red-gold glow so incineratingly close to us.

"Exceedingly," Tara says candidly. "When we plan our eruptions the most intricate testing is required for silica tetrahedron to determine viscosity of volcanic flow, to keep the magma very low in gas content to reduce carbon dioxide accumulation. The most stringent controls are placed on the rate of the thermal plume emitted by release of our lava so it won't produce a pyroclastic flow—"

"A what?" Joss asks, and I bless her for the question because I have just barely managed to follow Tara's explanation thus far.

"A boiling cloud of ash. Built-up pressure explodes it out with hurricane force, with hot ash so heavy it chokes and coats and clogs and buries everything. It's what blew out of Mount St. Helens in the twentieth century and when Mammoth Mountain exploded, when Mount Hood devastated the Pacific Northwest."

"Our water supply," Joss says. "We don't know how long we may have to be here. With the water for hundreds of square miles all poisoned from the toxins—"

"It's what's making this whole idea feasible." This I do understand, and I'm happy to be the one to explain it. "We know that ancient lava sometimes formed in layers as it cooled and we were hoping water might be trapped deep in these layers, separate from the contaminated aquifer, a substantial enough supply to support our Unity. We're continuing to test, but so far we've found enough pools to serve us for a century or more."

Tara returns to her charts while the spectacle outside the viewing panels fully absorbs Joss and me.

Later, as we prepare to return in the gopher cart, I finally understand how we are dealing with one, at least, of our two critical problems. The concept of creating a volcano is so deviant that who would suspect ours is anthropogenic? Its eruptions appear random and unpredictable, and the lava flow, small by historical standards and seemingly not atypical, appears unstable enough to warrant only aerial observations—why would anyone, even the most dedicated volcanologist, come to this contaminated place? The dramatic steam clouds afford us some cover, and in carefully calibrated combinations we feed the debris from building our site into the caldera as continuous fuel, solving the related problem of disposal, a process that can extend well into the future because we have unlimited fuel. The lava will spread out over the land, sealing it, forming a clean mantle over the contamination. Over time the lava will break down and form a healthy crust over this leprous lesion, one of too many on the body of our beleaguered Mother Earth...

The problem that exists within ourselves over living here—that is the one that now seems the most burdensome. And formidable.

2200.3.15—AFRICA

Day one of this journal. A record I keep for my purposes and for the future benefit, if any, of the Sisterhood. To this date there has been what has gone before this journal; and there is now. Two parts, no resemblance.

Maintaining a journal has always been a necessity for me, never an indulgence. The stringent restrictions placed on what we could bring with us to this habitat were of concern to some of my sisters but not to me; I immediately slid the microchips of these chronicles of my life and work into a shirt pocket and, like all my sisters, incinerated all else in my dwelling, leaving no physical trace of my former presence. My life has been my work, and my work has been my life. Had I not needed the microchips for a purpose, I would have destroyed them along with everything else without hesitation. Had the Sisterhood not needed my continuing existence, I would have long since extinguished it as well. Without hesitation or an iota of regret.

In the world we abandoned, there were others like me, others in my profession of synthesist. We inhabited a netherworld of information extending beyond a universe of computers, the collators of the collated, distillers of essence. My colleagues were all specialists in narrower fields of knowledge, none of them a generalist like me. My journal entries are but a further reduction of essence, in a sense the synthesizing of synthesis—unvarnished truth that speaks for me and to me alone.

I have painfully, grievously missed this time each day. After a day of all-consuming activity absorbing and assessing a myriad of detail, the intimate privacy and basic simplicity of my own mind has always been solace, a refilling of spirit, the simplest, most calming, most meditative time of my life. But I have been too preoccupied to record in my journal, enmeshed as I am in the tumult and urgent necessity of planning and swiftly building and protecting our new world, and my every spare moment away from my main decision-making duties has been filled with the imperative of examining my previous journals and scouring my memories.

In the outside world I was Africa Contrera, councilor to the most powerful of the powerful. Over the past seven months my fame has putrefied into infamy. I have shouldered the burden of limitless, unmitigated, unpardonable guilt. As I must.

I did not seek succor, but esteemed Olympia and Isis took it upon themselves to insist on giving me counsel. In summation: "This is not your doing, nor is it your fault. Your logic regarding this level of culpability is flawed. You are irrational. Let our psychotherapists assist you with your perception." But there is no possible mitigation of my guilt. In the depths of my being I know the truth: that I failed ignobly in my profession when it was most urgent, most imperative that I call successfully upon my abilities. And beyond that, I am a criminal. A war criminal. Without question I will be pronounced as such by history. Who would see this more clearly and uncompromisingly than a synthesist?

There is no rationalizing the stark truth that I aided, in

full measure, a man whose evil is literally without parallel in the recorded history of human beings on this planet, and beyond all comprehension by any sane person. I strengthened him. I gave him, unstintingly, the totality of my talents.

I am haunted day and night by the specter of him and by the grim question: How could I not have known?

Further: How could I have not seen so much as an indication, the smallest hint of his monstrous potential? How could I have so misread him?

Having already committed the grossest possible misjudgment, I am crushed under the burden of knowing that I cannot, must not fail again. Survival of the Unity on Earth may hinge upon my assessments.

Thus far I find no clue, either in my journals or other existing textual history, or in ransacking my personal memories, to the greatest, most urgent questions confronting our Unity: What is his eventual aim? What will he do next? To what extent will he search for us? Accurate prognostications are essential to our self-defense measures; our Unity's need for them is vital.

If I could identify the genesis of the man's monstrous conduct, this would generate analyses of his strengths and weaknesses, extrapolations of his future acts, and would point us toward successful defense stratagems, perhaps even allies on the surface world.

Thus far I can offer nothing beyond the minimal conclusion that his behavior will continue and will be no less unpredictable or inexplicable. Also that he has surely determined that some of us remain here on Earth, and he will likely expend every effort to find us—tenacity was a legendary characteristic of his before any of this happened. Although I have not spoken of it, I know he will divine that I did not depart for the stars with my sisters—he knows me as well as I know him. Truthfully, given my misjudgments of him, he knows me better.

Theo Zedera is a psychopath. What else can I call him? His actions fit—to heinous excess—the classic clinical definition: an antisocial personality disorder manifested in aggressive, perverted, criminal, or amoral behavior. My quandary is that contrary to all previously proven tenets, he does not fit into the classic behavior *profile*—a distinct arc of escalating, compulsive violence, a predictive pattern that was exhaustively documented well into the mid twenty-first century before successful treatment was implemented. Today we know that such fatally damaged personalities are always obvious by age seven, always identifiable by brain exegesis, and that without cell infusion combined with psychotherapy they proceed from stage one arthropod torture to stage seven serial homicide and mayhem. Which is not to say that we have eradicated such personalities; it is an open secret that they are sought for recruitment by certain world leaders who find their services useful and convenient.

How could Theo Zedera, however deviously clever, hatch into a full-blown psychopath overnight as if from an egg? Without undergoing physical or chemical trauma, without ever having previously shown a single identifiable symptom? So abnormal a brain pattern could never have eluded the brain function scanners guarding the entrance to all the halls of power as well as educational, governmental, and medical institutions. A man frequenting the highest echelons of governance as he always has could not possibly circumvent the scrutiny given such individuals. That I can neither explain nor define Theo Zedera causes me to question my own perceptions and sanity.

I have known him all my life, and all of his. Born a week apart—myself first—in the same neighborhood in Nairobi, inseparable childhood friends, we were opposites who somehow fit together, yin and yang, light and dark. He, sturdily built and fair; I, slight of frame and brown-skinned. Our dark eyes—the color of ebony—our one element in common. In competitive lockstep march during all our years of schooling, as academic rivals we challenged and pushed each other more than any teaching protocol or parental or authority figure possibly could. He with quicksilver clarity of mind and passion for argument, a charismatic personality drawing people into line to follow him; I no less passionate in my arguing of ideas, but the more quiet strategist, addicted to the pure joy of assimilation of entire realms of information and developing my gift for integrating and then parsing the mass of data into pithy meaning and, finally, forming predictions based on that assessment. We pursued our complementary fields, his in the broad field of sociology and governance and mine in the far wider disciplines that would lead me to synthesism. It required no leap in logic to understand that if we continued to work alongside each other, our career trajectories would ascend together.

It is agony now to remember how intellectually close we were, as affectionate and quarrelsome—and trusting—as brother and sister. Sexuality never factored. We discovered very early that we had another commonality, exclusive attraction to women. They were drawn to him easily, as if to sun, and he enjoyed them just as easily. As for me, after a few fleeting relationships that left me desolate, I saw that it was not in my nature to have dalliances that held no hope of a fullness of connection, and I was too absorbed in my consumption of knowledge, too absorbed by my career to offer anyone so small a part of myself, so bleak a future. For these reasons I spent more hours and days of my life with him than with anyone.

The ultimate irony: He was a prime reason I chose not to accompany my sisters to the stars. He was so close, so precious to me, so irreplaceable that I could not bear what would be the equivalent of death: losing him from my firmament. If I could no longer be a part of his life and career, at least I could observe from afar and not be separated from him forever.

Reason tells me that this could not possibly be so, but it was as if my withdrawal from him released some toxin that overnight turned him into a monster: the dreaded Zed. Butcher of nations. Of cultures. Of all freedom.

I am a synthesist of world renown, yet I cannot begin to assimilate or comprehend the dimension or causation of what has occurred.

In a scant six months his savagery has surpassed that of Hitler, Stalin, Zhou, Pentroni—everyone, all the arch-fiends of history combined. He has conclusively proved that the ultimate efficiency of modern weaponry is also its ultimate fallacy. After the Indo-Chinese biological war, even the dimmest thug of a dictator understood that all-out use of atomic and biological weapons would present him with a barren, empty, and contaminated earth to rule.

That was before an altogether new weapon was fashioned.

That was before medical DNA banks, created for the highest and most noble of purposes—to treat every illness of every human on the globe—were raided by Theo Zedera, and all their compiled DNA codes copied, the banks then destroyed. That was before DNA scanners, perverted from their legitimate use for identity confirmation, medical diagnosis, and health maintenance, became instead instruments of assassination, their first targets the world's leaders and their advisers and successors, rendering virtually every major nation leaderless.

That was before satellite-originated laser fire. Before narrow beam lasers, set for precision stunning or killing or vaporizing, could atomize parts of cities or whole cities, and wide beams could disintegrate entire countries—these weapons inspired by a so-called missile defense system dating from twenty-first-century America, a purported nuclear shield they nicknamed Star Wars. All of the destruction neat and tidy, with no radiation, no toxins, just the ashes of disintegration and precisely incised black patches on Mother Earth where people and nations and all their centuries of history used to exist.

Theo's Zedera's coup was as flawlessly carried out as if I had planned it.

And I had.

The potential for the world being held hostage by a group of fanatics has existed since the conception of weapons of mass destruction. That a relatively few perfectly placed operatives, loyal to a strong leader, could override any failsafe system has been true of every single weapon of horror. The scientists Edward Teller and J. Robert Oppenheimer, central to the creation of the atomic bomb, were the first to lose their naïveté, to be appalled by the dimension of what they had facilitated. The seeds were there and have always existed for a power base of fanatical followers, a chosen few zealots intent on earning the leader's approval by carrying out his orders with an excess of efficiency, however lethal. But precisely how these systems could be compromised, precisely where those operatives could be placed, was information I gave to Theo Zedera as a danger to be *nullified,* never imagining, never dreaming of how he would one day pervert it...

I was the one to provide him with the concept and blueprint of a theory. The key, which I handed to him in specific detail, was that given DNA data banks, given laser weaponry, a coup of worldwide dimension—a takeover of all the world's governments—was feasible if leaders were eliminated, if the most significant military installations were destroyed completely and without warning, and if the base of operations could not be identified or traced. And if the coup were executed swiftly and flawlessly.

While we were able to receive transmissions from outside our valley, before the major ones were cut off and taken over, the greatest agony I have ever known was witnessing his implementation of every detail of my theory—beginning with the looting of the DNA data banks and the destruction of those banks as their information flowed into his hands. At the same time came precise vaporization of key military installations on every continent and in virtually every country with significant land mass. His final execution of the coup fulfilled every definition of the word *merciless*. Iraq and Poland, having immediately replaced their assassinated leaders while other nations were still milling in confusion, were the first to step forward and refuse the demand for unconditional surrender. Without further warning, they were vaporized. Switzerland, its banking group representing itself as government in absentia, announced that as had been its historical custom, it would remain neutral. It too was vaporized.

At this point a news blackout ensued, successfully designed to foment worldwide panic before a central information bureau was installed to disseminate the official version of the news. For a time we received a type of shortwave transmission common during the twentieth century, and we still intermittently do. From this we learned that all other opposition—and at first there were many pockets of foolishly brave resistance—was being snuffed out with equal ruthlessness. We learned that scars remained as stark warning: blackened patches on all the continents. Some of China and South Africa and a significant portion of the Ukraine are gone. Segments of the Middle East. In North America, much of British Columbia, Texas, Nebraska, and Colorado have been obliterated, as have parts of other states. Theo Zedera took no live prisoners. Why would he? The entire Earth was his prisoner.

And I did this. All of it.

He claims no national affiliation with our birth country of Kenya or the continent of Africa. He truly never did. One of his first acts of political awareness—he was nine years old—was to reject the theory of nationality based on country of birth and to express contempt for any patriotism that extended beyond a sentimental fondness for a land mass. A position my sisters and I share, since tribalism combined with theism are clearly responsible for every war in history. I believed what he told me, persuaded that his belief emerged from an idealistic embrace of freedom—the antithesis of the tyranny he has now imposed.

Official estimates place the toll of the laser attacks at nine hundred million casualties. *Casualties.* The universal euphemism for dead human beings. Nine hundred million human beings are dead, and the concomitant carnage to Earth and human culture is inestimable. Theo Zedera is the most obscene individual in the history of Earth.

And as for myself...he is the one reason why I live. To find the key to this man, and the means for our Unity to survive him. Perhaps even to find a means of exterminating him.

Night or day, I can sleep for no more than an hour before I am awakened by my torment.

Theo Zedera, familiar to me as the palm of my hand, whom I loved so well—how could I not see in him this malevolence, this savagery?

To this day, to this moment, I can only see the gentle, piercingly intelligent, idealistic leader—my childhood friend, my lifelong friend, my trusted confidant.

A man I loved and trusted with my life.

And worst of all, a man I trusted with the secret of our Sisterhood's existence.

2201.9.15

Over the more than two years since the Takeover, Lucan Desmond had learned that Zed's taste invariably settled on places such as this one, a mansion "on loan" from its hapless owner, as were all the houses the Premier fancied. A lovingly restored twenty-room house dating from the seventeenth century, situated high on a hill in wintry Quebec City, it overlooked the winding cobblestone streets of the old city on one side and the St. Lawrence River on the other. To Desmond, this predilection for homes from bygone eras seemed at odds with Zed's unsparing annihilation of carefully preserved, nonthreatening historical sites such as Moscow's Red Square, the Parliament Buildings in London, the Capitol in Washington, Berlin's Reichstag.

In the room set up for the conference, Desmond tossed his attaché case onto an ivory-inlaid table priceless in its materials and design, careless of whether he damaged its delicate surface. He was bone-tired—he would not take a stim until just before Zed made his appearance—and he took in the splendid twilight view of the river's icy blue flow with a perfunctory glance. Sitting to the right of where Zed would preside at the head of the table, he adjusted the formachair to a cushiony consistency and a reclining position as it conformed to his body.

He was intentionally early; five subordinates had been newly, suddenly elevated to the status of general, and he had not finished reviewing their briefing or the most current summaries relating to the Disappearance. Although the term "current" these days suggested a mutable definition. The data, an endless flood, poured in from so many sources and was laden with so many false leads and tributaries that the best synthesists this side of Africa Contrera labored inhuman hours to quantify and authenticate it. The Premier's demands for updates came at any hour, and he expected instant and thorough briefings and seldom accepted any statement, conclusion, or overview at face value. Woe betide any general who tried to slide by Zed's searching questions about that general's territory with anything less than thoroughly detailed analysis and full grasp of its import.

Staring sourly at the oil paintings of historical Canada—Desmond much preferred modern audio-motion scenes, not these dry, static depictions Zed so admired—he sighed. In these intervening two years since the Disappearance, the event was top secret by classification only; the time had long since passed when details and troop movements related to the search could be kept under wraps, however dire the punishment meted out for leaking official government information. The military's fruitless hunt for the escaped women had become a source of snickering—albeit clandestine—derision to the world at large, and "sightings" of the women escapees had become a cottage industry of clever misinformation, and, beyond that, a lethal guerilla warfare weapon, the first effective rearguard action against Zed since the Takeover.

One of Desmond's elite strike forces had been lured

into the Brazilian jungle by a seemingly confirmed sighting of a community of women and cunningly forged photographic evidence, including an apparently genuine bio-signature match. His men had been ambushed and gassed before they could erect force fields, before any rescue extraction could be launched, their bodies clubbed into unrecognizable bloody pulp. Another team had been similarly induced into the Arabian Desert, its calls for rescue descending into a series of screams as it was tortured with slow, armor-piercing laser-pistol blasts before the entire unit was incinerated.

Desmond's orders for sorties into uninhabited expanses of country continued to be obeyed to the letter by his commanders, but the troops had begun to make gruesome, whistle-in-the-dark jokes about what dire fate might be awaiting them, and there had been other, more minor incidents, also excessively cruel in execution—unmistakable messages of rage over the Takeover and hatred for Zed. In each case severe retribution had been taken on all suspected collaborators and all adjacent territory, but in practical, specific terms it was futile: The actual identity of perpetrators remained unknown. The most current rumor had it that the vanished women were themselves involved.

Desmond gave this rumor no credence. But the Disappearance had been accomplished so efficiently, the ensuing search so fundamentally fruitless, that he found himself speculating on whether all the women might have escaped on their ship—might have managed, despite the limits of their ship's specifications, to cram in an extra two thousand or so passengers; might have figured out some way to bend universally accepted, supposedly immutable laws of science.

He dared not risk broaching this to Zed; he would

blister Desmond with ridicule, citing the universal equation that proved the women's ship carried no more than 4,200 voyagers because of its weight/escape velocity, plus the axiomatic formula that oxygen and food processing capability rendered impossible a viable flight beyond the Einsteinian Curve to the Arcturan system and the first planets for a viable landing outside the solar system. Still, however ridiculous his theory might seem on the face of it, he would no longer put anything past these women, including the creation of any technology needed to achieve their ends.

He had done exhaustive research into their low-visibility lives and was impressed with their range of talent and accomplishment. Perhaps they had built a second ship, this one somehow eluding detection as the first craft acted as a decoy. A scenario possible, however, only if the women had discovered a way to remain invisible from high definition solar system scans.

Desmond's ruminations were interrupted by the arrival of three black-clad operatives carrying detectors and spray guns. "Apologies, sir," one murmured, and the sweep team deferentially bowed and began to back out of the room, but he waved impatiently for them to perform their duties.

Silently, swiftly, they completed their scan of the room for toxins and bacteria, then sprayed the walls and windows with transparent Fluxbar. With more bows, they withdrew to await the Premier and his aides before applying the substance to the door as well, sealing all discussions in this room from probes of any kind.

Who was left to attempt any such probe, Desmond wondered irritably. And for what purpose? The Premier was in full control, had crushed his opposition with such ruthless efficiency that all visible dissent had vanished.

Who dared speak openly when merely the slightest hint of criticism—it did not have to rise to the level of insurrection—brought immediate reprisal? The Premier did not require that his local lieutenants bother with niceties beyond an informal inquiry before issuing a punishment order—a destruct command given for a specific DNA sequence, carried out the next time the condemned person or persons passed a DNA scanner, and scanners had been installed everywhere, simple machines simply programmed to destroy their targets and/or the source of any attempt to destroy or disable them. Suspected dissidents, when identified by a scanner, were bathed in laser fire and vanished into swirling dust molecules. As were their associates, sometimes their entire neighborhoods. Some were selected for torture—the unluckiest taken by Esten Balin—their broken bodies displayed on national vidscreens and hologram stands.

Were the women themselves somehow able to tap into the Premier's highest-level discussions? Was that why they had so effectively eluded capture? He shook his head. He was getting paranoid.

Desmond's five new subordinate generals, resplendent in their dress whites for their first audience before the Premier, filed past the DNA scanner and into the room. They were, of course, unarmed and had been fully screened for toxins. He returned their salute without rising from his chair, then opened his attaché case, flipped on the wall and table display units, and prepared to get to work.

An hour later, as Desmond and his full complement of twelve generals stood at rigid attention, Premier Zedera walked into the room, Esten Balin strolling along behind him, stim-cigar in hand, his gaze fixed on the lowering sky and the river beyond the windows. Eight gray-uniformed aides also entered, to stand in absolute stillness with hands clasped behind their backs beside the food dispensers, ready to spring into action at any order for food or drink the Premier, Balin, or the generals made on their signal pads.

"At ease, gentlemen," the Premier said softly. He absorbed the view beyond the windows for a lingering moment, then moved briskly to shake hands and welcome the new generals as Desmond introduced each one.

The Premier took his seat at the head of the table, Balin to his left. As everyone else relaxed into their formachairs, several of the generals signaled to the aides for the liquid refreshment of their choice, and Desmond brushed a hand across his mouth, unobtrusively ingesting his stim pill. The room quickly filled with the aromas of rich cigar smoke and the seductive fumes of the latest concoction of alconarc.

A good sign—both Zed and Balin were dressed casually, the Premier in the soft, shapeless clothing he preferred, Balin in tan military pants and a black turtleneck sweater. A bad sign—the Premier had greeted Desmond with cool distance, and Balin had not acknowledged him at all.

After a toast to the new generals, the Premier set down his wine goblet and asked, with a hint of sarcasm, "Does anybody have any good news?"

Kenan Vartan, one of the new generals, was rotating his wineglass between his thick fingers. Into the silence he offered drolly, "We have a few more leads."

"Wonderful news, General Vartan," the Premier remarked, and chuckled; and after a beat everyone joined in. Desmond directed a grin at Vartan, awarding him points for his impudent courage.

"Let's begin," the Premier said.

"Area six, report," Balin barked.

"Yes, *sir,*" General Stephan Gruber said eagerly. He straightened his shoulders, his fingers dancing over his pad; figures and animated graphs emerged in holograms on the table, a confluence of past and present data, with extrapolations.

Area six was Eastern North America. Desmond looked on with interest, always intrigued by Zed's focus on a particular territory, always seeking clues to the mysteries of the working of his mind. And Gruber, though ambitious to a fault, was also bright and energetic.

"Economic convulsions continue. With the monetary system having less and less relevance. The black market and barter are now a common means of exchange—"

"We have area lieutenants all in place?"

"We do, sir. We're collecting our share. Water is becoming the main component of the barter system. Access to fresh water continues to be the primary cause of unrest. You can see the numbers, sir. Even with the most stringent conservation of all supplies including rainwater, available supplies have shrunk to minus two point seven-five critical—"

"What price on the black market?" the Premier inquired.

"Depending on the quality, a high of one hundred and fifty credits per pure barrel in New York City down to thirty for industrial grade."

"Up five from last month," the Premier observed, without expression. "Continue, General."

"Overall situation: calm. Only fourteen hundred executions last week, sixty-seven hundred for the month in the sector, down sixteen percent from January. Significantly, three conspirators disseminating false information about the Disappearance were made into a very public example over a three-day period—"

"Where? Who were they?"

"Massachusetts, Boston." Gruber tapped his recorder, then read off the names of three women as their images appeared on the display units, all of the women young and dark-haired with bold dark eyes.

If Gruber expected to be praised, he was disappointed. "Sisterly solidarity. How foolish," the Premier said with a scowl. "False information related to the Disappearance—remove it from the proscribed list. No further punishment."

Amid a dismayed murmur from around the table, Gruber protested, "Sir, it's our only protection from the mass of misinfor—"

"It's no protection at all, General."

"May I speak in loyal dissent, sir?"

"Speak."

"Our imposition of a universal death penalty turned out to be a most effective deterrent against dissent. All opposition has been—"

"Yes, against dissent. But review the data related to the Disappearance. Informants can make their electronic tracks so intricate that the few culprits you manage to isolate and execute only prove investigation to be a thorough waste of time and resources."

A waste of time and resources, Desmond reflected sourly. Far and away the most egregious waste had been the time, men, and materiél squandered on solving the Disappearance itself. None of the vanished women's DNA sequences had been entered into the scanners for destruction—the Premier wanted them alive—and deliberately fake bio signatures were always triggering false alarms. And to what end, all this—for what purpose? A purpose known only to Zed, and never to be questioned, exemplified by the five generals who one week ago had considered it their duty to circumvent Desmond and raise this question directly to Zed. They resubmitted the contention—previously rejected out of hand by Zed—that the women must have perished in the high casualties resulting from the Takeover, and challenged his continuation of the search. A disintegration command had been issued, and they had been automatically and summarily and very visibly executed by DNA scanners as they left the Premier's compound.

Desmond had no sympathy for the five. Had they first—and properly—discussed the question either with himself or Balin, they would have been saved from themselves. They had deserved execution for their stupidity.

The Premier said to Gruber, "Don't officially announce that punishment is off your list, General. Deterrence, for whatever value you place on it, will still continue for a time. The sociological trends and data now, please."

"Yes, sir. By far the most popular form of entertainment continues to be the viewing of ancient motion pictures..."

Uninterested in the latest demographics on this phenomenon, Desmond gazed out at the St. Lawrence River. There was nothing new in Gruber's report. People, in groups large and small, were obsessively watching holographic representations of old films, not for the story or the acting but to marvel over people feasting at tables laden with a vast quantity and variety of foods, hunting animals not for food but for sport; people catching fish, using precious fresh water for *bathing* instead of wearing clothes treated with bacteria eater. People driving fossil-fuel cars, going to libraries filled with books made from trees, tending herds of cows grazing vast expanses of green, arable lands. Activities impossible for anyone born in the past century to possibly experience.

Except for people like himself. He enjoyed the most luxurious of surroundings, the finest of food and drink, the most voluptuous of women. The Premier did not permit weapons of any kind in his immediate presence, would not allow profanity, nor did he wish to witness the mistreatment of women; otherwise he placed no limits on the behavior of his circle of advisers and generals. Desmond sensed that the Premier noticed and valued his comparatively temperate appetites. Desmond enjoyed intoxicants but did not have an addiction problem, and his encounters with women were fleeting pleasures. He could not have children. He saw no reason for a permanent relationship or for any deep involvement.

Desmond's attention returned to Gruber, who had switched topic: "Narcotic consumption continues to escalate, especially among the youngest percentile of the population—"

"Demographics?"

Desmond, the stim continuing to sharpen his senses, observed the tall, slender, blond Gruber. Always watchful amid the shark-infested waters of his officer corps, Desmond was especially aware of Gruber, whose aristocratic bearing was a veneer camouflaging rapacious ambition. Gruber could scarcely tamp down a coiled certitude that given an opportunity he would prove that his ideas and leadership skills far surpassed Desmond's.

Laser pointer in hand, Gruber moved gracefully around the display unit and provided crisp narration of each of the nine drug categories as he went through graphs that seemed to dance as they formed and reformed in vivid color codes. Stable rates of narcotic consumption continued among the oldest population group, representing sixty percent of the citizenry, code color purple; significantly higher consumption among the middle-aged thirty percent, code color red; steeply rising rates among the youngest ten percent, code color green.

"Gender?" the Premier asked.

Another graph emerged, code colors pink and blue. "Ninety-seven percent skew toward the male gender, up from eighty-eight, sir."

Desmond heartily approved of unrestricted legalization and the open accessibility of all narcotics and the Premier's order to make them freely available—after all, the ultimate opiate of the masses, beyond religion, was even more opiates. But he could not fathom Zed's obsessive interest in tracking every specific of what seemed an obvious outcome.

"Economic production?" asked the Premier.

Falling, Desmond thought. What else could occur? The fallacy of drug availability as a major controlling device was the continuous intoxication of a significant proportion of the population—ergo, a significant loss of human-based productivity.

Gruber ran through a full fifteen minutes of highly specific data covering increasing dependence on robotics to compensate for declines in the agricultural and service economies, before concluding, "Productivity continues from the older population, which has taken on the role of village elders to fill the leadership vacuum. But even with robotics productivity has fallen to five percentage points from the median stability level."

"Thank you, General," the Premier said in dismissal.

"Sir, I would like to bring to your attention some facts about religious attendance and conversion."

Desmond looked sharply at Gruber, alerted by the sudden eagerness in his voice.

The Premier also was studying Gruber. "Proceed."

Gruber brought up new graphs in a formation across the tabletop. "Since December, religious conversion is up thirteen percent. As you can see, the predominant sect continues to be Baptist by four point two percent, but—" He highlighted a silver column with his pointer. "—cult formation and membership are rapidly closing the gap. The cult numbers are highly significant—"

"*Highly* significant?" Balin broke in. "Why should anything about these cults concern us?"

Desmond, seething, stared at Gruber, who had not made eye contact with him. There was no reason why Gruber should not have covered this development with his commanding officer before broaching it with the Premier. This opportunist had gone too far. This piece of excrement had obviously been waiting for this moment.

"The cults certainly should concern us," Gruber replied to Balin's question. "One sect in particular, and one man in particular: Ferdinand the Messiah."

The roomful of men laughed. Even Desmond couldn't help chuckling.

"Tell us about the fearsome Ferdinand," Balin said, grinning around his cigar.

On the viewscreen, images formed of a stocky blond man with a full beard, piercing blue eyes, a hooked nose, a wide, thin mouth—rotating images of him ranging from full-face to profile to the back of the head.

"His cult is called the Shining," Gruber said doggedly, grimly. "His compound is in Alabama, membership is male only—"

"Homos?" Balin asked.

"Anything but."

"All the homos, I don't get it," Balin ruminated to the room at large. "We got way more women and fewer kids than ever and more homos."

"This isn't the time or place for sociological trends and historical anomalies, Esten," the Premier said mildly. "Although it's my field and I enjoy discussion. Continue, General Gruber."

"Mr. Balin makes a good point, sir. Satellite reports show the Shining to be exclusively, militantly heterosexual, male supremacist, Caucasian only. Shaved heads, white robes, daily chanting rituals, very heavy into all varieties of aphrodisiacs."

Gruber clicked his pointer and the viewscreen filled with a scene of what he had just described; the room resonated with the sound of drumbeats and guttural male chanting. Gruber cut off the sound but not the images. "Ferdinand the Messiah has all the magnetism characteristic of cult leaders, and a belief system fundamentalist in the extreme."

Gruber allowed sound again, and the bearded man screamed into the room, "Birth by sperm! Death for birth control! Death for abortion!"

"We execute women when we have to," Gruber commented, "but this is the first religious sect since the Dark Ages to advocate the burning of women."

The bearded man screamed into the rising cheers of his audience, "Death for unnatural procreation! An unnatural child is a monster! Death to monsters! Any woman using Estrova—we *burn*! Anyone *found* with Estrova—we *burn*!"

The images faded and Gruber turned off the viewscreen. "The sect is growing at about ten thousand a day."

"I happen to agree with good old Ferdinand right down the line," Balin rumbled, grinning around his cigar.

And he'd fit right in with his shaved head, Desmond thought. Along with fearing Balin, Desmond loathed him.

Balin, disdaining his signal pad, beckoned with a raised

hand, and an aide scurried over with a purple concoction in a crystal goblet. Balin swilled most of it, then said, "We make the laws—most everything this fanatic wants is already a law. No birth control, no abortion, no children created from Estrova instead of sperm. So who cares? If a few renegade women get the Joan of Arc treatment, so what? It'll help keep the rest of them in line. They burned anybody yet?"

"Not yet, sir. I doubt they will."

"Then why should we care about this bunch of chanting nuts?"

Gruber looked gratified, if not delighted, by the question. "Because the Shining is spreading like a virus, sir. Ferdinand the Messiah is taking full advantage of the Premier's generous allowance of complete freedom of religion to disseminate his message by hologram projection everywhere meetings are held."

He clicked his pointer and illuminated the viewscreen. "As you can see, in effect he's in the same room interacting with drug-intoxicated and highly suggestible men. But this isn't a collection of drunken lunatics. These are ordinary men who want to believe what this man preaches. That the spreading use of Estrova means the freedoms given to women have created every evil in the world. Are contrary to God's will. Have brought God's punishment to men. Ferdinand the Messiah says repent, atone. Accept this punishment and the punishment to come, accept a life of ascetic discipline, bring women into line. Wait for the day of atonement. He's preaching this gospel of righteous supremacy to men who feel inadequate and powerless right now, even with our guarantees that the situation is temporary. We project the Shining will reach over six million in membership in the next three months alone."

His pointer light gleaming on the graph showing this projection, Gruber earnestly addressed the Premier. "Mr. Balin asked why we should care. The major issue for us is this: Ferdinand the Messiah's overarching theme is that the end of the world is imminent, and that his followers and his alone will attain a higher plane."

Desmond smiled. Gruber would end up with minimal gains for his gamble. Bottom line, this was just another doomsday cult.

But Zed, his powerful shoulders hunched over the table as he leaned forward, looked intrigued. "This doomsday scenario," he said. "Does he give a time frame?"

"No, sir. Not yet. The psychologists I consulted unanimously predict naming a date and stating a definitive outcome will be the final step in consolidating and then galvanizing his followers toward whatever cataclysmic act he wants from them."

Gruber took a step toward the table to emphasize his next point. "I know your orders are to permit any and every exercise of organized religion, but the Shining fits the profile of a cult with high potential for mass homicide or suicide or both. And with millions joining—"

"Nonsense," Balin said. "They—"

The Premier waved him to silence. "Do you have a recommendation, General Gruber?"

"A precision strike, sir. Ferdinand the Messiah and the key members of his innermost circle. Because of your generosity in allowing any and all religious observance, we couldn't use DNA scanners, and we'd have to take great care in making this leader's death look purely accidental. Then trump up some charges of sedition against his lieutenants. Or, have Ferdinand's death be plainly murder and frame his lieutenants."

"Quite logical, General," the Premier said, nodding

slowly. "And very good work. Outstanding work. For now I want his actions monitored—nothing else. Arrange for infiltration. And dedicated satellite surveillance of his compound. You are hereby appointed to special assistant to the Premier and will report directly to me—and I'll expect your reports on a daily basis."

"Yes, sir." Gruber's alacrity was almost palpable.

Desmond heard the Premier's order in consternation. Gruber had won his gamble. This most dangerous of sharks—next to Esten Balin—had suddenly moved into the closest proximity to the Premier, a position where he could not be checkmated. And replacing Desmond would be his one and only goal.

2201.9.15—OLYMPIA

It has been just over two years since we abandoned our former lives. A time for reflection. For taking stock.

First, under the category of the Power of Unintended Consequences: this amazing chamber.

When our agronomist, Wilda, presented the proposal for its creation, the Unity gave unanimous approval based simply on the concept and placed it on priority track, judging its implementation to be essential not only for its healthy oxygenated byproducts of photosynthesis but for our morale and to add to the aesthetics of our world. Bringing their specialized talents to the collaboration in its design were geophysicist Rozene, biologist Hasana, and my own mathematician sister Isis, with her knowledge of vector geometry.

"Didn't I tell you how important and wonderful it would be?" Isis boasts to me every time we walk in here.

She did, in fact, but I do not believe for one moment that my sister ever imagined just how extraordinary it would be, just how profound its impact would be.

Located inside the Stein-Toklas Mountains at Faderman's View, its one-way observation windows look out on more than fifty miles of stark desert sky, a pinkish-tan playa of more than two hundred square miles containing a vast white salt pan—one of Earth's largest—edged by varicolored foothills harshly sculpted and contoured by centuries of relentless heat and scouring sand. It is magnificent, awesome; it is a haunting, soul-stirring sight. The chamber itself has been hollowed out of two hundred vertical feet of Faderman's View. We intend to expand both its interior depth, presently at five hundred feet, and its width, half a mile and rapidly growing, all along the surface contours of the mountains.

DNA has, of course, been the indispensable ingredient in making possible the life forms we have brought to our world, including those in this chamber. Certain equipment has also been vital—robots and processors for the making of ore. Thanks to Africa—who laid out all the orbital paths of the satellites, including oblique angles, and when imagery would be the least precise, and what activity would be spotlighted and reported as anomaly—we brought these supplies to Sappho Valley in a carefully planned operation. Rakel, piloting a freighter plane outfitted with counterfeit markings and appearing to be a routine unmanned flight to Vega, followed a low trajectory and jettisoned our supplies in one perfectly timed maneuver into a specially camouflaged tunnel equipped with a homing device. She also scattered miniaturized surveillors before she flew on, these designed to home in on and adhere to rock; those on the hillsides give us clear visual monitoring of much of our valley floor, except during blinding sandstorms.

Because of our circumscribed environment, we have had to introduce a tightly controlled ecosystem from our precious store of DNA samples from thousands of Earth species, and by selective cloning and forced-growth techniques.

Thus this great chamber, which we have filled to abundance with quickly maturing trees as well as birds, insects, plants, and small ground animals. Cats and dogs were, of course, immediately introduced to our world and have had the run of it from the beginning. Because we have included young redwoods, sequoias, and the ancient and noble kauri, we have given the chamber its soaring height to accommodate future growth, which we have accelerated; we light our forest for hours longer than natural daylight would on a surface habitat, and load our recycled watering system with nutrients. Indirect growth-lights filter and slant down through the trees and form lovely patterns on a forest floor softly carpeted with ferns, leaves, pine needles. The presence of a waterfall and of angiosperm imbue our forest with a feel of the primitive, the primeval—an atmosphere enhanced by hues more intense than those on the surface. Every shade of green, even of foliage in shadows, has an amber-toned sheen as if our forest were permanently touched by sunlight, and the rich smells are as loamy and fecund as if we're inhaling Mother Earth herself.

As our world's historian I dutifully asked Hasana about this amber tint on our foliage, but I must confess when she launched into detailed explanations of the chemical makeup of biomes and rhizospheres, my mind wandered. Some might contend that I am abdicating my duty as historian, but so be it. Like Mother, I too am bored by details, and further, Hasana keeps her own scientific records for anyone interested in such arcana.

To all of us, this place, which we have named Tiptree Forest, is no less than a cathedral...perhaps because it is encapsulated within Mother Earth herself, and therefore more intrinsically part of her. Some of us have gone so far as to agree with Tara's proclamation that she feels more like a cave dweller now than an underground inhabitant. Others, including my dear Joss, no longer complain that our forest-perfumed air smells "funny" but still insist on describing themselves as "sighted moles consigned to life in Earth's bowels."

Nonetheless, as the months flow past we have all become more assimilated into our world, while the exterior world descends deeper into chaos. Tiptree Forest marks a turning point in our all-out effort to build a secure home in Sappho Valley. Our habitat, still raw and unfinished in major respects because of the priorities of concealment and establishing food and water supplies, is beginning to bear some resemblance to our overall design. It is, however, far-flung, and gopher carts are more prevalent than ever with their high-speed underground transport of people and goods throughout Sappho Valley.

The hydroponics chambers and greenhouses, strategically located high in the eastward-facing peaks of the Woolf Mountains, are generally unaffected by the thick steam cloud from Bannon Crater during its active phases; the prevailing wind spreads it northeast out into the vast empty desert country known as the Great Basin. This mountainous barrier to our valley absorbs the sun's early-morning radiance and strongest energy and life-nurturing properties. The hydroponics units located there are heated and nurtured by the sun through apertures in the rock, openings that rotate to follow the sun's trajectory but appear indistinguishable from the surrounding indigenous rock. The units' nutrient solutions are constituted from the rich soils of the Central Valley of California, famous for containing nine of the ten soils to be found on Earth. Thanks in major degree to the agricultural experiments of our wondrous Wilda, we enjoy a varied diet of foodstuffs of high quality and intensity of flavor.

Most of our Unity comes to Tiptree Forest daily, after long and intense hours of activity. Singly, in pairs, or occasionally as a group, we walk, gaze at the vast horizon and majestic valley, sit among the trees to rest and to meditate. Some of us have taken to adjusting the color of our clothing to match the foliage in a kind of osmosis with the trees and ferns. Thanks to Africa's suggestion that use of the forest extend beyond the aesthetic, our youngest children play in their own designated area and are schooled there as well, to the delight of those lucky enough to be their assigned teachers—and of course we all participate in that happy task, as we do their parenting.

Occasionally, for those who wish such a ceremony, nuptials take place here too, with Isis or myself symbolically linking the hands of the women who seek the Unity's witness of their commitment to each other. With the use of Estrova, six babies have been born in the forest, two sets of triplets, Cantara naming the very first triplet to emerge Tiptree.

My sister and I, close all our lives and now virtually symbiotic, have an unspoken understanding that we desire solitude when we are in this place. For it is here that I live among my memories and—I know my sister so well—it is the same for her.

Two years ago Tara stood on the stage of our camouflage dome with Isis and myself, presenting the options for where we would make our home. I clearly remember how she shifted her laser pointer over to Australia and her words: "The Outback. Among the largest desert areas on Earth. Sacred land to the Aborigines, Earth's most ancient indigenous people, and however benign our intentions, we cannot include it in any equation of ours, we cannot intrude on their beliefs or their land..."

Had we been able to live on that continent, I would not feel any closer to my lovely, tender Celeste than I do here. Or any further away. I have loved many women in my century of life, and am fortunate enough to have been loved in return. But Celeste...

She is the love of my life. As I am of hers. But ours was a fusion of mind and body that could not endure the practicalities and pressures of spending our days and nights together. However much I attempted to shield her, this shyest and most delicate of creatures, she withered under the constant heat of having to be in the proximity of the Inner Circle, the unremitting visibility of being partnered with a firstborn of Mother's. So now my Celeste has fled from me to the stars, accompanied by her adoring and protective Nerisa—which is the prime reason I remain here with my sisters.

While I can fervently wish I were of a later generation and therefore a less prominent personage in our Unity, so that Celeste might have remained with me, I accept what is immutable and begrudge her none of her happiness with Nerisa. The distance between us has had the benefit of dulling the pain's keenest edge, but at night I so ache for her silken hair and her sweet, welcoming body, her gentleness...

She is somewhere in the universe, lost to me. I will always mourn her. At night, when my soul is sorely tried, I come here. Others of us, for other reasons, come to Tiptree Forest as well. In pairs. And I hear them. With a vast moonlit sky strewn with crystalline stars and moonlight casting immense shadows on the eternal desert beyond the windows, some of my sisters lie together amid the darkened, fern-shrouded depths of our forest; I hear their smothered sounds of ecstasy, their joy in one another.

Joss too comes here, in daylight so far as I know, and unlike her sisters she does not wander the forest savoring the play of light and the ever-changing pathways through the trees and ferns. She has a favored spot she climbs to, in the leafy branches of a young but sturdy oak tree beside the view windows. There she sits, her back against the tree trunk, creating music that only she, through her aural inserts, can hear; as I pass below her I can plainly see the hunger on her face as she stares out at desert and sky. I feel her longing for the life she once knew. We all feel it.

She is by no means the most troubled spirit here. Far from it. That distinction belongs to the woman who sits amid the ferns in the same place at the same time, unaware that Joss is nearby. Immersed in torment, in guilt-ridden misery, she endlessly searches her journals for clues as to how she could have so misread Theo Zedera and his potential to commit his heinous acts. She is by no means the "biological pathogen" or "Hitler's lieutenant" she calls herself. This particular cadre of monsters cooperated in mass murder with alacrity, and no one ever accused them of having morals or any capacity for conscience-based remorse. But no one can persuade her differently.

I am anxious about both of these women, and watch them. I've noticed in the past few weeks that Joss has become aware of Africa and awaits her presence in the forest, although she takes great pains not to intrude. More and more often, as I stroll unobtrusively past, Joss's gaze is fixed on her. And from how I read her face, it is a gaze of utter and unchanging compassion. Not unusual for or atypical of this descendant of mine who seems to blend sophistication far beyond her years with the bold energy of youth. Joss's infatuation with Tara seems to have faded...or perhaps my matchmaker mind only imagined it in the first place. Indeed, it is Tara who seems besotted with Joss. Perhaps, in the perversity of such things, it is because of Joss's seeming detachment around her, unlike our other women who seem magnetized by Tara.

I know Joss will never disturb or approach Africa. Few of our women do, and certainly none of our youngest women. They are more thoroughly intimidated by her than by anyone, including Isis or Tara or me. Only Mother is in

Africa's exalted category. Even before the tragic grandeur that surrounds her now, there was the isolating nature of fame itself: She was one of the most recognizable women anywhere in the outside world, and that aura has followed her here.

It occurs to me that I can use my own good offices in these circumstances. Perhaps bringing these two together in some form of meaningful work or mentoring collaboration might engage Joss more fully in the work and worth of this world and refocus both of them on the future instead of the past.

I myself am the best example of this. My work here is my consolation, and a most considerable one—what is left of my life has renewed value. I must confess that more and more I feel a burgeoning sense of adventure I haven't known in years, perhaps since I was a child growing up with my eight gifted sisters, when we were making our way into a perilous world under the affirmative tutelage of Mother. None of us could have dreamed that all this time later we would be part of the creation of a new society and the building of a new life. I am helping to build a world, and I am more useful here than I have ever been.

If only Joss and Africa could be made to understand this...a work collaboration may well be beneficial for them both... It is my hope that I can effectuate a change in viewpoint.

Joss is strong—strong enough to accept and withstand the force of Africa's suffering. For all her rebelliousness, there is an energy about her that will be good for Africa. Yes, they may well provide distraction for each other.

2201.9.22

Desmond and the full complement of his twelve subordinate generals were assembling with seemly haste around the table in the council room at the Premier's compound in Quebec City, having again been peremptorily summoned. Several of the men looked harried, among them Levor Copeland, who'd had to return from Africa; he had arrived only minutes earlier by supersonic jetpod and was now inhaling stim to recover his wits.

The haste of this gathering was not unusual, and Desmond was heartily sick of it. The Premier called his meetings without warning and usually with no more than a day's notice, and he had not rescinded his policy that absenteeism was not permitted; so it was left to the generals to solve any problem of being here. Among the Premier's officer corps no one thus far had tested the consequences of an absence.

Amid simultaneous salutes from all his generals, the Premier strode in, Esten Balin as usual trailing him. "At ease, gentlemen, be seated." He took his place at the head of the table, Desmond and Balin to his left and right. Stephan Gruber sat down next to Balin and smiled perfunctorily across the table at Desmond. Gruber had been at the compound the entire week instead of in his usual territory of eastern North America, and Desmond had been busy building a team of informers to keep him apprised of Gruber's activities.

"Supreme General Desmond," the Premier said, "please report."

Using his full title in front of Desmond's subordinates, especially the newest ones, was a good sign, as was the brief softening of Zed's face that was not quite a smile, and Desmond felt reassured that he did have the Premier's trust. He would keep it. He looked at his generals in their black uniforms trimmed in gold, the four small red bars on their chests subordinate to his five. Except for Gruber, the attention of these generals was focused on him in respect. The military was his to command. And an accident, a regrettable accident, could befall Stephan Gruber...

There was only one subject Zed ever wished him to report on, and Desmond was succinct: "All known associates of the escaped women have been permanently detained over the two-year period since the Disappearance. They have been questioned repetitively and exhaustively, using all means possible." He brought up a series of graphs. "Their physical and mental breakdown rate has reached seventy-seven percent."

He flicked a glance at Esten Balin, who was smiling complacently. Several of them had fallen into Balin's hands. Desmond pushed away the memory.

"In summary, what have we learned, Lucan?"

The courtesy in the phrasing of the question was for the new generals, but Desmond heard an edge. Bottom line, he thought, the escapees had simply vanished without a trace. As Zed well knew.

He began formally. "From all the data we've assembled, we conclude that they are of all racial mixtures. Overall they appear to have had little lasting interaction with anyone except one another. There are exceptions, of course," he added, carefully not looking at the Premier. Zed's lifelong friendship with Africa Contrera was public knowledge, and Desmond had accumulated in his private files voluminous additional documentation of its closeness. No direct evidence of sexuality between them, but Desmond took it as a given that there had been and that this was the reason, perhaps the only reason, for the obsessiveness of the search.

"Lesbos?" Balin inquired idly.

"Depends on your definition. They've had heterosexual couplings, but every durable relationship has been with one another. Before the Disappearance, while they were phasing out their withdrawal, they managed to obliterate virtually all evidence, even trace evidence, of themselves. Dwellings thoroughly fluxed—not so much as a nail scraping. Records altered or expunged. We only began to learn about them as the most famous among them disappeared—"

Desmond was prepared for the scowl on the Premier's face, which appeared at any mention of this aspect of the Disappearance. Zed's anger was undiminished that no one had correlated all of the individual disappearances until Africa Contrera vanished, one of the last to go. Clearly, the Premier believed he himself could have prevented it, persuaded her from her escaping.

"Ironically," Desmond continued, "these sanitized dwellings provided a commonality and have been our most reliable source for identifying and accounting for all the rest."

He had gone into summary overview for the benefit of the alertly listening new generals, who understood from the coding number on their keypad screens that this was ears-only information limited exclusively to those in this room. "The bio-signatures we've acquired are from weak traces, the result of painstaking sampling at the places where they performed their professions—"

"General," the Premier interrupted, "if I may have a word."

"Certainly, sir," Desmond said, taken aback.

"I have some additional information."

Desmond heard this in astonishment. In every conference or briefing, the Premier listened, asked questions, expressed opinions, issued orders; he never imparted information.

The Premier said, "It's time to advise you that the women involved in the Disappearance possess a genetic identifier unique to them."

No one in the room moved; they were fixated on the Premier.

"Billions of calculations and ensuing syntheses have traced this sequence back to a single origin..." The Premier paused as if to give his audience a chance to brace themselves, then said, "The unlawful late-twenty-first century mating of an Earth male with an alien humanoid female from the Arcturan planet Verna-Three."

His searching gaze fell on each man in turn as he continued. "Since Verna-Three still does not have space travel, this much is clear: The male was a member of the Space Service at that time, and he somehow smuggled her onto this planet. About the female we know nothing, other than her descendants refer to her simply as Mother. We've thoroughly questioned every crewman we can find from that era without results, but twenty-two percent of them have died or been lost in space in the interim, and in any event the crewman's identity is now basically irrelevant except to punish him. So, beyond these scant but certain facts, the identities of this original male and female remain unknown."

The Premier leaned forward and his voice lowered so that Desmond had to strain to hear him: "Genetic analysis proves conclusively that genes from the Vernan female would be dominant. Without exception, the pregnancies of every descendant of this illicit couple would result in a female birth, with multiple births common. These, gentlemen, are the women who fled during the Disappearance."

Along with everyone else in the room, Desmond had absorbed this information in stunned silence. But his thoughts raced. This was not, could not possibly be new information to Zed. He had been with Zed from the start and he knew all of his information sources, he knew every move Zed made. No investigation or program of genetic analysis could have been conducted without his knowledge, even though sociology and its allied area of genetics were Zed's special expertise. Operatives loyal only to Desmond covered Zed and his activities thoroughly. Zed had to have known this from the time of the Disappearance, if not before. He had simply decided to reveal it now.

There were two obvious questions. One was why. The five dead generals had to be a good part if not all of the reason, and Desmond sent a silent salute to the five. While they had paid the ultimate price for questioning the Premier's judgment, this challenge had led to Zed's decision to be forthcoming as to the real reason behind his granite determination to solve the Disappearance. The second question was: Where had the Premier received his information? An interesting, indeed fascinating question. Perhaps this was the Africa Contrera factor...

Desmond stared at the Premier. At the compelling face that magnetized attention, the hypnotic dark eyes that pulled the viewer into their depths but revealed exactly nothing.

The thirteen other men lining the table were still frozen

in place. Collecting himself, Desmond spoke first, and with feeling. "This is a catastrophe. We need to renew—"

"How could it happen?" Balin demanded amid a voluble outburst from around the table that Desmond's remark seemed to have loosed. "Every female returning from space always went through full scans. Despite their never-ending howls of protest."

The Premier raised a hand for silence and said, "The best guess—the only guess—is that the Vernan female took the place of a male crew member."

"A catastrophe," Desmond repeated. "This is exactly why we had to prevent interbreeding with aliens."

Galvanized, Gruber was feverishly punching his keypad. "With multiple births, using a factor of three as a reproduction rate they could increase to millions...tens of millions. They could reach critical mass in another ten generations or less!"

"Well, they're not all that clever, are they?" Balin growled, stabbing ash off his cigar. "They were well hidden in the general population but made the mistake of revealing themselves."

"Why?" Kenan Vartan asked. "Why would they do this?"

"Yes," said the Premier, nodding at Vartan. "What conceivable reason would they have for leaving this best of all possible worlds?"

Amused by the sarcasm, Desmond knew better than to show it because the Premier did not.

The Premier said, "The best guess is that a breakaway faction wanted to leave, forcing the others who wanted to remain here into hiding."

Desmond said, "I have an idea. Why don't we offer them amnesty?"

"Because it's a *stupid* idea, Lucan," the Premier

snapped at him. "We'd have to do it publicly. And they wouldn't accept anyway—these are smart women."

"Maybe they went back to Verna-Three," said Vartan.

"They did not," Desmond stated. "We've scanned all previously visited and inhabited planets. But that may be their eventual plan, and we should maintain surveillance."

"We'll find them. We have to," Balin said. "And the ones in space too. We'll exterminate them." His fist closed crushingly around his goblet. "In a manner I'll design myself, appropriate to these women."

2201.9.17—JOSS

I can scarcely believe this day.

"Awe-inspiring" is the least anyone ever says about Africa; of all the extraordinary women in our Unity, she possesses the most extraordinary genius. Her work in our Unity amounts to no less than identifying and defining every potential flaw in every process affecting our entire habitat and our odds for survival.

Her evaluation of just our construction plans and architectural theory assumes a breathtaking familiarity with the most minute detail of all the related areas of geophysics, biology, volcanology, topology, morphology and hodology, hydrochemistry, and hydroponics.

Her tact in the performance of her work, her modest reticence in the face of universal admiration are legendary, as is her quiet manner. She suggested to us during our basic design phase that we "might look at some nonlinear interconnections between the corridors..." and that offhand observation produced the revisions in plan that meant much more efficient transportation between our tunnel spokes and the far-flung areas of our valley. There were many other suggestions, particularly in her area of governance, but many of them were the microscopic kind that made subtle but important differences in our daily lives.

Just recently she made a casual suggestion about our children's nurturing: "We might give them their own place in Tiptree Forest." Which resulted in possibly the key transition phase for them from the outside world to this one.

It's not all that long ago that I received my own mothering, and it came from many in our Unity besides Silke, my birth mother. Here the children receive similar loving care—but from newly designed and far more expansive circles of us now that we are all together. I too am part of three of these circles, reveling in the care of our children as I learn more of the complexities of motherhood from those older and more experienced than I. Our philosophy of family is being implemented with far greater freedom—and more inexpressible joy—than was ever possible in the outside world, where we had to conduct ourselves with caution so as not to attract notice or suspicion or hostility, even though ours is the logical approach to nurture and produces strong, confident, self-sufficient women—women like those in our Unity. The kind of women reviled in the outside world, from all we hear on the brief, intermittent short-wave transmissions that tell us about increasingly repressive laws and even antiwoman cults.

We are fully implementing our philosophy of education: Children accompany each of us on various days during our routine activities, and our instruction of them is built around the intricacies of these activities. So I am learning to be a teacher too. It was within this context that Africa made her suggestion—which has led not only to their own endlessly diverting area for play but to the creation of an elegant onsite laboratory for the older children's studies and experiments in ecology.

Charis and Autumn have asked Africa informally for her opinion of the noncritical parts of our agenda—their unfolding programs in art, literature, and music. So she's involved herself in this too, in addition to the ongoing analysis of work on our defense perimeter. But everything she does is secondary to her major priority.

"Defense is paramount," she contends. "At some point our survival will depend on the quality and precision of our preparations. Sappho Valley will be investigated and searched thoroughly, regardless of the volcanic hobgoblin we've created in Bannon Crater."

We have no cause to doubt her prediction—does anyone on Earth know the capability of our enemy better than Africa? She has come to us with ingenious nuances for our defense preparations, which we have adopted, as we have many of her ideas. Even so, she has no authority beyond the force of her intellect and her credibility—nor, of course, does any one of us. Tara coordinates our activities, and we have agreed to accept her arbitration when disagreements become hardened and adamant, an occurrence by no means rare. Consensus, in fact, seems by far the rarer commodity. Just yesterday argument raged throughout Sappho Valley over the ecological ethics of how the desert comes into play as part of Africa's defense methodology.

Having been involved in this wearying discussion, I complained irritably to esteemed Olympia, "How can we call ourselves a Unity when we clash and argue constantly?"

"Passionate discussion is our strength, our greatest strength," she reminded me.

We do sharpen our intellect, principles, and solidarity, our wits and humor against the whetting stone of open and unfettered minds. But ours is not a utopia. Intellectual conflict is open and can be exhausting.

Understood among us is that we may always appeal beyond Tara to esteemed Olympia or Isis. Since they are the ones who recommended Tara to us as coordinator and arbiter, such an appeal would require circumstances—or folly—beyond my imagination.

In any case, Tara considers consultation with Africa mandatory for any decision of importance, and since Africa's assessments have been proven acutely insightful and accurate, an outsider might logically ask: Why isn't she our de facto leader and arbiter instead of Tara?

"Leadership is a gift that Africa does not remotely possess," esteemed Olympia told me bluntly. "She offers immense knowledge and directions to solutions, and gives them willingly in service to her sisters, but she is unable to marshal that talent toward issuing decisions, much less edicts."

A giant in intellect, regal in her bearing, her dark hair a soft nimbus around her face, she is small in stature, deferential, shy, self-effacing. Yet arresting. She will walk into a noisy room as unobtrusively as a shadow, and every time women will sense her presence and fall immediately, if momentarily, silent.

We all know she is haunted by her decades-long allegiance to the most evil man in history. Some of the reaction to her can also be counted against what Olympia calls "the incandescence of fame." But mostly it's because the torment in her is palpable. To see a smile on Africa's face is the rarest of occurrences, and it's a perfunctory and polite business when it does happen. In all the time she's been here with us in the Unity, I can't recall ever having heard her laugh. The aura of tragedy that accompanies her isn't visible in her posture—she always stands erect, her shoulders straight—but is weighted in her eyes, eyes fathoms deep in their darkness. They have a luminous sheen of intelligence that seems to surface from a core of pure, burning anguish.

She is haunted. And I too am haunted. By her. I have

always been. Long before Theo Zedera turned into the marauder and butcher of nations, long before she carried the weight of his horrors in her soul.

She is the great secret of my life, the secret I've confided to no one. Granted, not having a soul ever suspect how I feel is hardly a feat, since I have the great advantage of being able to freely express unstinting admiration of Africa just like anyone else.

But all the time she and Theo Zedera were rising meteor-like through the ranks of diplomacy to the international stage, when her image adorned historical and contemporary records and flashed over Earth's vidscreens, I watched her avidly, watched both of them, these traveling ambassadors between the world's leaders. Zedera front and center, magnetic, charismatic, while Africa shied away from her renown, resulting in the perverse consequence of an endless obsession with her in the world media.

I shared the obsession.

Awareness of her reaches into my earliest childhood. I remember my birth mother, Silke, remarking about her high visibility, that it presented a grave risk to the secrecy of the Unity. When Mother judged her contributions a cause of hope for Earth, that ended the discussion. Mother could not have known that in the ensuing years, while Africa Contrera was famously facilitating our Unity's ideals of disarmament and cross-cultural integration and equality as the pillars of governance, Theo Zedera was collecting the knowledge that would lead him to become...Zed.

I understand why Africa believes that only she could have foreseen this deadly potential and prevented it. I understand why it is her unendurable burden that she did not. That I disagree with her does not matter.

I have read and viewed everything concerning Africa.

This is no exaggeration. Everything. And have retained that record in triple-coded privacy on my own personal datascope. Amid all my close connections with friends and family, all my intense infatuations with girls in my immediate circle, nothing overrode what is in the core of me, what pervades me. To this extent: My beloved birth mother expected that I would accompany her and my sister, Trella, to the stars, but I delayed my decision virtually to the deadline and could not satisfactorily explain my procrastination. I was waiting for Africa to resolve her own agonies of indecision. When she decided to stay, her choice was my choice. I no longer had to worship from afar. I could be close to her as never before. For my amazed and grieving family, I did my best to make them understand that this is where I needed to be. I hold these hopes, however insupportable: that life is long and I will see my mother and sister again; I will find them again one day in the stars. In the meantime I will be near Africa, where I need to be, and nearer than I ever dreamed possible.

From the beginning I understood that I must maintain absolute secrecy about her. I was astute enough to realize that revealing my thoughts and feelings would result in structural and theoretical analysis of my brain and psyche for incipient delusional obsession, and the monitoring of my access to any information whatever about Africa Contrera. No one would give credence to my assertion that I have no hope or expectation of any reciprocation from her. I have never tried to contact her, have never come near her, not even at gatherings of the Unity when I was in her proximity. The delusional person is the first to say that they are not delusional, but I have passed every test measuring the center points of my rationality. I have always known in my very fiber that my feeling for her is not from sickness—it is in fact from the highest and best part of me.

In the world we left, I had begun to receive recognition for the ethereal music I create from jets of air currents, and in my world here I am regarded as a musician of fine poetic sensibility. My music has all been inspired by Africa. It is my inexpressible joy that when I do perform here in Sappho Valley, she is in the audience, never dreaming it is she I perform for, that she is my muse.

What holds me so compellingly? It is what I saw in her the very first time she came into my vision, which was probably on a vidscreen or as a hologram when I was five years old—long before the millstone of Theo Zedera began to attach itself to her soul.

I saw her loneliness.

Ineffable sadness has always, always emanated from the Africa I see. I see an Africa whose fame has imposed isolation upon her. An Africa for whom loving connections can never be fully formed or trusted because of the world stage she occupies and the demands of performing on that stage.

Why did I choose to remain here? What do I want from her?

Nothing, unless a continuation of my phantasm counts for something. There is nothing I want to take from her.

I have been told I am strong. And I am, both physically and emotionally. I am not strong enough—no one is strong enough—to take her burden from her. But I long to somehow be able to consecrate my strength to her. To lift that burden from her for a day, an hour, a moment—I know I am strong enough to do that, and strong enough to require nothing in return. I dream of giving her the simplest comfort. Being closer to her now than I have ever been, I long for it more than I ever have.

But reality is a force that blows more harshly than our desert winds. And fantasy is no more than a wisp of cloud in our desert sky...

Then a day ago esteemed Olympia took me aside. “Tara has approved my asking: Would you like to assist Africa?”

To be even closer to this woman if I wished it? I was so overcome I did not know what to do with myself or what to say. “Assist her?” I stammered. “What do you mean? What am I supposed to *do*?”

“Be useful,” Olympia said tartly, fixing me with the gaze of unmitigated impatience I deserved. But then, seeing how genuinely undone I was by this prospect, she added, “Anticipate her needs. No one can ease her emotional burdens—we all know that. You can be there to do anything she can delegate to you, even if it’s locating minor pieces of information to save her time. If all else fails, Joss,” she concluded with exasperation, “you can just be there to pick up her recorder if she happens to drop it.”

Finally, there came the brilliant dawn of realization: This was my dream. My dream.

Struggling to control my voice as joy overwhelmed me, I nodded. “I would be honored to serve her, esteemed Olympia.”

2201.9.27—OLYMPIA

The association between Africa and Joss began with the meeting in my chambers where I had summoned the two of them, and with Africa saying to Joss, "Olympia has explained that you are willing to assist me, but I'm not sure how—"

"Africa," Joss interrupted, "I will find many ways to be useful to you."

Africa looked startled enough that it occurred to me that few people ever interrupted Africa Contrera. Then there was a brightening of her face that these days passes for a smile, and she reached for and took Joss's hands. "Thank you," she said.

At Africa's touch, Joss could not have looked more stunned than if she had been struck by lightning, and she remained fixed in place until Africa released her hands. Then Joss said calmly, formally, "I took the liberty of determining what you prefer for your noontime meal, and have organized it for you. Transportation awaits your next appointment, which I've learned will be at the hydroponics unit."

So began my experiment to put Joss and Africa together. It has been most interesting. Beyond interesting. Intriguing.

Most observers—and there are many interested observers, quite notably Tara, whose attention seems siphoned to these two whenever they are in her presence—describe them as polar opposites. I would define them more as a potpourri of qualities and attributes. Joss is solid yet so supple in her movements, in that stage of lovely awkward grace some physically strong women pass through in the final stage of growing into the fullness and vigor of their bodies—her awkwardness more manifest and captivating when she is around Africa. Africa, while slight of stature, is abloom with a consummate maturity and assurance and more energized and engaged around young Joss, beyond even what one would expect from someone so preternaturally gifted.

Over the years, I have come to know Africa well, or at least as well as anyone except for Theo Zedera, and have come to see that there are two personas. The one who puts on a public face of quiet serenity when forced to deal with her success and fame, and the private one, whose modesty and self-deprecation—once upon a time there was impish, teasing humor as well—are genuine, who is at heart quite a shy woman, and endearingly so. But something I have never seen in her emerges when she is around Joss: an ever-so-subtle preening. Not that Africa is aware of it—and not that it removes for a moment any of the burden she carries. Still, her self-absorption has been diverted by this young woman, a development that has given Isis, Tara, and me cause for hope that the psychological forecast given to us by Helene may yet prove inaccurate.

A forecast of ninety-nine percent probability for suicide of course surprises no one and is of precious little use to us. Should Africa choose this path, we will not and cannot prevent her from exercising the fundamental right to put an end to her pain as she chooses.

Given this context, I am gratified by my matchmaking ability. More so because it did not come out of our unspoken tradition of carefully assessing our young women and arranging for them to be in proximity with those with whom they share interests and sensibility. This practice has by no means eliminated or even discouraged relationships based on brushfire sexual attraction, nor the emotional devastation at breakups, but it has resulted in many highly compatible and happy pairings over the decades. I can't imagine Joss and Africa in a romantic situation, brushfire or otherwise, nor, I suspect, would anyone.

What Joss offers is the universal attractiveness and energy of youth, a pleasure to us all, but finite and limited, especially when measured against the infinite depth and variation of Africa's sophistication. What matters is that in the short term Joss's youthful optimism is beneficial to Africa, pulling her away from herself. I have no doubt that over the long haul it would grate against the self-containment at Africa's solid core.

That Joss and others of our young women resent our living circumstances comes at least partly out of the nature of youth; circumstance and necessity have thwarted their natural adventurousness. It is their immature, although fully legitimate, view that the course of their lives has been chosen and imposed upon them.

What surprises about Joss is her sheer willfulness. Unlike the rest of us, she has not succumbed to the aura of Africa and her genius, and the effort behind Joss's determination that she will not be intimidated is almost visible. I search in vain for words to describe her manner when she is around Africa. I can safely state that she is deferential and solicitous but fiercely protective. The other day I witnessed no less a personage than Tara having to confront Joss at the entrance to Africa's quarters: "Move aside,

Joss. Her standing order is that I am to come to her immediately with any question of urgency—"

"Is our valley being invaded?"

"Of course not, but—"

"Then it's not urgent. I don't care what she's told you," Joss stated, hands on her hips. "I will not allow you to disturb her. She's tired, she needs to sleep whenever her mind and body permit it."

I was about to intervene to try to save the situation from becoming a reportable incident of insubordination when Africa came up behind Joss. "I'm awake, Joss, thank you," she said. "What is it, Tara?"

As Tara took Africa's arm and drew her down the corridor, I noticed Tara's glance at Joss. Not the angry glance I expected, but one deeply wounded. I also saw the look Africa gave to Joss, the gratitude and the softening in her dark eyes.

With all her solicitude, Joss does not fawn over Africa, common behavior toward her by some in our Unity who should know better. Nor does she appear infatuated. Yet "protective" does not entirely describe how Joss is around her. I must also use an old-fashioned, virtually obsolete word: She is courtly. But there is something additional...something I can neither precisely identify nor describe, but Africa has responded to it, and that's what is most important, not my poor definitions.

If Joss has distracted Africa from herself, she has not diverted her from her work. She and Joss have been focused on the holographic elements of our inner perimeter defense, Joss helping to set up and then assist with the laboratory models and the myriad tests.

Which brings me to this moment. Tara, Isis, and I wait in the small conference area off the holograph lab for Africa, who has requested a meeting, an unprecedented event that can only mean the issue she brings to us is grave.

Tara seems relaxed enough, however; she has reclined her chair and waits with a booted foot up on a carved rock ledge, threading the fingers of one hand through her fine blond hair as she reviews a report that has come in from Wilda. Tara's hours are so lengthy that like Africa she recaptures strength and energy by relaxing her body wherever and however she can. I realize that not only is she calmly regenerating herself under these ominous circumstances, she is also being a leader. A leader with the self-confidence to believe she has the resources within her and around her to successfully address any problem, who therefore sees no reason to anticipate disaster or to show uncertainty or apprehension.

My sister, however, looks as worried as I feel. I wonder if I appear as worn-down, as bent-shouldered as she does by our unremitting peril, our living under the Sword of Damocles that hangs over our valley. There are times when my century of life weighs heavily on me, when I give in to my deepest terrors, when I become acutely aware of the fragility of our little band compared to the leviathan arrayed against us. We live within Mother Earth like a child in a womb, trusting to her protection while our enemies relentlessly prowl her surface, seeking to destroy us. If they find us, what can happen is so horrific that my entire instinct is to demand a suicide contingency plan.

But of course I cannot. In my position within the Unity my duty is to keep my gaze focused forward and not look up at that metaphorical sword over our heads. I know I cannot hint at my fear, much less broach any of it to any member of the Unity and thus undermine the spirit and optimism around me, the determination that we will survive and flourish and one day see an end to all this. I know we must continue to build our home and protect it in so thorough a manner that we can live our lives fully and with confidence.

Only Isis knows my fears, and she reaches to take my hand as if she has read my thoughts. After all our years together perhaps this sister of mine, who is my closest friend, has indeed done so. Dear, dear Isis, with a face so noble and beautiful with age. She squeezes and releases my hand, then plucks at and tidies the folds in her royal-blue robe...

This gesture is so familiar to me, familiar since the days of our childhood, that I cannot help thinking back to those exhilarating times. And understanding that we are in no more danger now than we were back then. If Mother's true identity as an off-worlder, an alien Vernan, had been discovered, if the authorities had learned that she had been smuggled onto this planet by our Earthman father, we would have been captured, used for lab experimentation, and then exterminated with no less ruthlessness than anything Zed could devise. Mother's resourcefulness in concealing our existence from official records until our numbers dictated that our genetic readings could blend in with the population at large, her optimism in preparing us to live in what she considered a barbarian culture—those qualities are now required from Isis and me, and the two of us owe it to Mother to emulate her, especially that confidence... But still, if Mother considered the Earth of those days a barbarian place, what would she think now? What would be her attitude, her approach to our crisis? I know very well what she would say, and I hear her voice as if she were in the room: *"I know you girls can manage."*

This time I reach to Isis's hand and squeeze it. "We'll be fine," I say, and mean it. Isis, the younger of us two by five minutes, smiles, and I can see that, for the moment at least, she too believes it.

Africa has entered the room. As always, I know it

without looking up, as if the very molecules of air have frozen for an instant, magnetized by her presence. Slender, elegant as always, she wears her synsilk trouser suit in the earth-toned colors she rarely alters, but there is something unusual about her: She carries only her personal recorder. No telepad, no stylus—items that seem an extension of her body, that even when she dines she is never without.

"Esteemed Olympia, esteemed Isis, dear Tara," she formally begins in her low, musical voice after she has gracefully seated herself. "I need to go out onto the desert surface."

So this is what it's about. I feel relief. Until I realize that what she proposes is impossible. If she were captured...

"Why?" Tara baldly asks.

"To verify the effectiveness of our holography."

"Why?" Tara asks again, shaking her head. "We've run hundreds of tests, Africa, we've got multidimensional imagery from our monitors—"

"Insufficient," Africa returns firmly. "We require on-site verification of verisimilitude and precise adjustments. Our imagery cannot completely duplicate the human eye, and the slightest defect will reveal our purpose."

"I will send—"

"No," Africa says. "I am the person best equipped to make the necessary judgments and assessments."

She is right, of course. But as I look into Tara's face, and then into Isis's face, I see that we are all united in our resistance.

"You could be captured," Tara says flatly.

Africa inclines her head slightly. "Yes."

"Any human life is an anomaly on this desert's surface." Tara's voice has distinctly sharpened. "Surveillance satellites—"

"Tara, who could know the dangers from the satellites

better than I?" Africa asks softly. "I will be appropriately cloaked. The probability that I will be discovered is ninety-nine point nine-nine percent against."

"Which is less than a hundred percent."

"Indeed. I will have a suicide contingency—I will carry the materials for my disintegration, of course." This last voiced with the same eerie calm as if she had said she would take water with her.

Isis has been gazing fixedly, acutely at her. "Without arguing the point of whether this is necessary, Africa, is there another agenda? Is it your plan, after you perform your verification, to destroy yourself out there?"

"It's an idea," Africa says after a moment, with the same eerie calm.

"A less than optimum idea," Tara says in deliberate understatement, with a half-smile.

"Far less than optimum," I chorus.

"Your work here is not finished," Isis says.

"Perhaps not."

This is a woman who has so accepted her unworthiness to live and her self-imposed death sentence that in her purview it no longer contains emotional weight or value. From the expressions on the faces around me, Isis and Tara feel the same dismay I do.

Then inspiration strikes. "Joss must go with you," I blurt.

"No," Africa says quickly. "Esteemed Olympia, I don't need her or anyone else to risk accompanying me."

Tara has been studying my face and Africa's. "Of course you do," she says, and it is a command.

Lifting both hands, Africa protests, "That will only increase the danger that so concerns you."

"The probability is exactly the same."

Africa looks at Isis with those turbulent dark eyes. "I

have assessed your suggestion that I kill myself out there, esteemed Isis—"

"What?" Isis gapes at her, aghast. "It was not a suggestion!"

A ghost of a smile quivers on Africa's lips. "Nevertheless. I offer you my personal guarantee that I will not destroy myself while on the desert surface."

Clearly, Africa is arguing, in her indirect diplomatic fashion, against Joss's accompanying her.

"Thank you for that assurance," Tara says. "But it is imperative that you take Joss with you. Something could happen in the desert that has nothing to do with the search for us. You could be injured."

After a moment, Africa nods. "You are correct," she concedes.

"You will bring her back safely, Africa," Tara says in an even tone, and it is an order and not a question—and the matchmaker within me perceives for the first time the true depth of feeling toward Joss that Tara has been at some pains to conceal.

Africa focuses on Tara the searching gaze that misses nothing and assesses everything. "I make you that promise, Tara," she says quietly. "She will return to you safely."

2201.9.30

All of the floor-to-ceiling windows in the Premier's compound in Cabo San Lucas were open to the day. A hundred meters away, sunlight glinted off the surface of the water and turquoise surf cascaded into a bright white carpet of foam. Premier Supreme Theo Zedera, wearing a soft white shirt, dark slacks, and velvet slippers, stood at the windows with arms folded, gazing out at the waves, his broad back to the generals who were fussily assembling around the council table, ordering drinks and settling themselves.

Lucan Desmond, who had seated himself in his usual place near the head of the council table, unfastened the collar of his uniform to savor the soft tropical air perfumed with heady ocean brine. Even the cigar smoke from a scowling Esten Balin, seated across from him, did not detract from the freshness and beauty of this day or these surroundings. Life was good, and if it weren't for the Premier and his dark moods and endless obsessive demands, it would be even better.

He had worked hard all his life, had given full commitment to learning military science and strategy and command, and then to each and every assignment. In effect he had been married to his career. There would come a day when all this work would end, when the Disappearance would be solved and the Premier's plan fully implemented. Desmond's dreams were vivid, and he longed for their realization: his own quiet tropical island with a climate like this one, and a beautiful compound like this one, and women, lots of them. And if they used Estrova to produce children, well, who would know, who would object? He loved his vision of an entire island of happy women, happy children, running, playing...

Desmond watched the Premier, trying to gauge his frame of mind; watched him turn away from the windows, arms still crossed, to look at the group. Tension accumulated in the suddenly quiet room as he contemplated each motionless man, including Desmond and Balin, in turn, with an unblinking dark gaze of evaluation, his expression, as usual, unreadable. Then the Premier walked to the ornate chair at the head of the table, an aide hastening to pull it out for him. At a nod, another aide fingered the controls for the windows, which silently formed an invisible sheet fully muting the thunder of the surf.

"General Gruber," the Premier said.

"Sir," Stephan Gruber said cautiously, rising to his feet.

In the intervening months since Gruber's impromptu performance in Quebec City, Desmond had not been able to determine whether Gruber's attempts to undermine him in private meetings with the Premier had succeeded to any degree; the Premier's confidence in him seemed unwavering.

Looking back over the ten years since he had met Theo Zedera, Desmond perceived that Zed's manner toward him throughout that time had basically never changed. Zed had recruited him into the inner circle of conspirators during the nonstop and fruitless diplomacy efforts to avert further Indo-Chinese bioterror and more millions of casualties. Desmond had been sick at heart over the carnage, in despair over his futility, and had not hesitated to commit himself and the Peacekeeper troops under his command, never doubting their loyalty. His troops were just as cynically weary as he of being impotent bystanders, armed eunuchs, pretend soldiers whose plumaged presence did nothing to prevent the protagonists of war from pursuing their ends, which included blasting the Peacekeepers out of existence when their presence became inconvenient. Zed had understood their impotence, had persuaded Desmond to join the coup and implement a blueprint that would lead the world once and for all away from the endless cycles of war. Desmond had given his trust to Theo Zedera and the grand design that would impose order and transform world governance and all of history going forward.

As a procreating man I'm impotent, Desmond thought, *but I've shown my potency as a soldier for Zed, and for all history for all time.*

Desmond could not be certain, but it was likely that the Premier, who possessed the shrewdest, most far-reaching and subtle mind Desmond had ever encountered, had seen through Gruber and gave credence to nothing beyond the value of Gruber's information. The information, Desmond conceded, was good. Very good. Gruber was devious, insidious, and exceedingly dangerous, but he was also exceedingly astute. No matter how thoroughly Desmond debriefed this renegade general before gatherings like this one, he had not been able to box him in; Gruber always managed to carry something extra into these meetings and claim afterward to Desmond that it was information he had developed or thought of at the last minute.

But perhaps not this time, Desmond thought, smiling to himself.

"General Gruber," the Premier said, "since you're the only officer here who seems proactive in seeking new information instead of regurgitating old news, the only one who ever offers anything beyond the routine and the ordinary, I'll begin with you."

Desmond looked up to see grimaces on the faces of his other generals, and Balin's open exasperation at the Premier's acid remarks. So he too was being worn down by the Premier's endless browbeating and relentless pursuit of solving the Disappearance.

"I hope to continue to merit your confidence, sir," Gruber said in an unconvincing display of modesty. "An important development: Residual effects of the Disappearance appear to have filtered down to an increasingly significant number of women planetwide. They've developed their own methods of nonparticipation and even subversion, not by means of a disappearance nor by a work strike, which they know would bring repercussions, but through what can best be described as...inertia."

"They're on strike?" growled Balin.

"More like lethargy. A work slowdown, sir."

"How? How do they pass the word? We control communications—"

"Word of mouth. Same as they spread Estrova. They've formed some sort of chain to pass on information."

Desmond had witnessed this himself, in the women who seemed less and less efficient if not downright inept in running systems designed to support his military, but it had happened so gradually—like the women who had phased out their Disappearance—and had seemed so intrinsic a part of the general deterioration that he had to give credit to Gruber for assembling the sociological evidence.

"To paraphrase that ancient maxim," Gruber was saying, "you can lead a woman to work, you can even make her work, but you cannot make her work well, or care about work."

This information was so significant that Desmond had expected demanding questions from the Premier, but he merely nodded. Puzzled by Zed's seeming indifference, Desmond speculated that perhaps he would return to the topic later in the meeting. He frequently did, as if the information he had received were percolating in a separate chamber in his brain.

"What else, General Gruber?"

"I have new reports on the escalation and proliferation of drug use and especially gambling—"

"Perhaps later for that. Ferdinand the Messiah. Supreme General Desmond suggests that you may have developed some further intelligence."

Gruber cast a surprised glance at Desmond. Enjoying himself, Desmond sat back and gave him an encouraging nod. "Am I not correct in that surmise, Stephan?" Desmond's operatives had become gratifyingly efficient in their infiltration and scrutiny of Gruber's activities.

"Yes, sir, I do have updated figures and of course intended to present them," Gruber said with enthusiasm, obviously making the best of things now that Desmond had stolen some of his thunder. He tapped his keypad. Several graphs formed on the table, along with holographic images, aerial views of vast encampments. "Cult membership continues to rise exponentially, in line with my previous projections. The Shining's membership rolls now stand at two hundred and sixty million."

Murmurs spread through the group. The cult numbers

had risen dramatically each week since Gruber had revealed its existence, and Desmond, who did not agree with Balin's casual assessment that Ferdinand's control over the cult was in effect a convenient surrogate control mechanism for Zed's central government, had privately expressed his own grave concerns to the Premier.

"More than a quarter billion," said the Premier calmly. "An impressive number."

"Even I have to concede that it's huge and going out of control, Premier," Esten Balin said. "It's a dangerous cult, a dangerous number. They have the potential to vie for power."

"Ferdinand the Messiah does want power, Esten, the power to control behavior," said the Premier. "But he's not interested in *political* power. Plus, they're spread over five continents."

"Correct, sir," Gruber said. "In virtually exact proportions."

"And we control transportation and we have the controlling weapons. Those who have the controlling weapons control those who don't."

"Factions are forming in opposition to the Shining," said Kenan Vartan from down the table. "I just returned from Pakistan and that brushfire that broke out between the Shining and the Muslims—it's indicative."

Desmond asked casually, "Ferdinand has just set an end-of-the-world date, has he not, General Gruber?"

Gruber sent him another surprised glance, this one containing vexation. "He has. We don't know what it is. No one does except Ferdinand's innermost confidants, a group of five we are not able to penetrate and on your orders have not approached, Premier. All their meetings are Fluxbar-protected."

"It may be the right time to take one of that inside

group and perform information extraction," Balin said.

Looking thoughtful, the Premier sipped his red wine, rolling it in his mouth as if taste-testing his answer. "Yes," he said. "Indeed it is time, Esten. Do so."

Desmond was relieved. Finally, finally the Premier was pursuing a course of action against this proliferating and clearly dangerous faction.

"Stephan," Balin said to Gruber, "you have a suggestion who we extract? I personally will handle the interrogation."

Meaning, Desmond knew, pain-enhancing drugs in combination with the most exquisitely prolonged tortures. Before he could forcefully push it away, his mind was inundated with an image of one of Balin's victims, what was left of a man bound on a table, shrieking, his skin flayed open, with Balin, his erect penis engorging the crotch of his pants, at work on him with his instruments. Anyone unfortunate enough to fall into Esten Balin's hands would divulge any information simply for the privilege of dying.

"I do, sir," said Gruber. "That would be—"

The Premier raised a hand. "I don't care who it is. I want it done immediately and I want it done right. The extraction must be flawless. You are both to cooperate fully with Supreme General Desmond, who will coordinate a plan to extract this civilian in a manner that will arouse no suspicion that the military is involved. I will tolerate no mistakes. Am I clear on this?"

Balin shrugged his acquiescence.

"Yes, sir," Desmond said, delighted.

"Yes, sir," Gruber said, and if he was deflated, and Desmond knew that he was, he hid it well.

"One other item, sir," Gruber said, and Desmond looked at him alertly. Was there to be a surprise here, after all?

"We've identified an enclave in the West Virginia mountains. We're uncertain of the numbers, but it's at least a quarter of a million homosexual males, forming their own community."

"How good of them," Balin said, hunching forward, grinning. "How convenient. Best news I've heard in weeks. Let's fry the whole lot of them. Better still, let me design an appropriate—"

"No," the Premier told Balin.

"Why not? We're infested by these—"

"Exactly. It's hardly all of them, Esten," the Premier said. "We wait. Don't you see that all of these birds of a feather are flocking together? We wait."

Desmond heard this without surprise. The chaos the world had sunk into over the past two years had all come to pass exactly as Zed had laid it out when they had planned each step of the coup, and even though the Disappearance had been unforeseen and a grievous distraction, Desmond saw no reason to doubt Zed's vision. That he did not fully understand Zed's plan in all its nuances was due to his own limitations. Indeed, he did not even begin to fathom every detail of Zed's overall scheme to impose order and tranquility, to eventually return prosperity and material progress to the world. Zed freely answered any and all questions, patiently and with specifics. Over many evenings spent with Zed at whatever palatial home he had commandeered, evenings of sensual splendor amid beautiful and acquiescent women, evenings of music, entertainment, and every conceivable intoxicant, he had heard Zed hold forth on innumerable topics having to do with world governance, with trade and commerce, with science and art; and the man's intellectual scope, his sophisticated grasp of facts and their essential meaning, were unmatched in

Desmond's experience—and he had been around the great leaders of great nations in his military career. Zed's ruthless seizing and consolidation of power were necessary; brutality was always justified when there was no other way to implement a larger vision.

"That will be all for the moment, General Gruber," the Premier said. "Please submit your full report for my review, and please highlight the information on women and work." He nodded to Desmond. "Continue, Supreme General. The complete historical search data I requested, please."

Desmond tapped his keypad; a huge representation of Earth hovered above the table, rotating slowly, as neatly segmented as a peeled orange. Red points of light, signifying the location of troops, pulsated in erratic patterns, intersected by a network of overlapping lines of green—the patterns of satellite reconnaissance.

"Just as I thought," the Premier said. "Over the period of the search, you've concentrated troops in all populated and tropical areas."

Was he being critical? The oceans and deserts had been subjected to surface and subterranean probes, every island on earth had been ransacked. Because the Premier refused to allow entry of their DNA codes into the scanners for destruction, logic dictated that the women had concealed themselves amid a general population mass, or in jungles where the terrain itself could afford protection. And Zed had been kept fully—*fully*—informed of all the search patterns.

"Yes, we've focused the search," Desmond informed the Premier. "But satellite probes and detailed comparison imagery continue over all land mass and ocean areas. We're overlap-mapping and analyzing every anomaly in surface detail on the face of the planet every forty-eight hours—"

"Converge satellite range," ordered the Premier. "Focus

ultra-high-definition scans on only the largest uninhabited areas, including the oceans, and increase pass-over intervals to every twenty-four hours. Ground forces?"

Desmond picked up his laser pointer. Zed had recently ordered wide deployment, a strategy Desmond deplored and had argued against as strenuously as he dared. A show of soldiers and weaponry to intimidate, restore order, and reinforce local control was sound tactics. But using testosterone-enhanced troops for peacetime mop-up and search operations when they were primed and stoked to fight an enemy of equals, held high negatives. In the economic chaos that now reigned, men were flocking to join the military, but even so his forces were stretched thin over wide areas, and they could not be restrained from committing mayhem. Their atrocities had won them nothing but hatred and were getting them killed. The revenge ambushes and torture killings of his men were wearing on morale—his as well as theirs. His men were loyal and dedicated in their performance of a difficult job in service to a larger vision, and he cared about them.

Pulling his thoughts to the matter at hand, he quoted data on troop strength. As he touched the globe with his laser, a column rose from each red point, illustrating the location where his troops were deployed and their numbers.

"What about these areas?" the Premier inquired, indicating territories void of red points.

"The oceans, where we have fully completed soundings—"

"Obviously."

"Outer Mongolia, the Sahara, the Australian Outback, the Great Basin—"

"Yes, all of it desert, clearly."

"We've swept through it all, sir. Total ground surveillance except for sections of the Great Basin—"

"Yes, the Great Basin. History?"

Desmond froze the holographic Earth's slow spin, entered a code, and took the Premier though the entire history of troop deployments and searches in sector sixty-nine in Western North America.

"Eastern Calivada, section three-two-A," the Premier said musingly, immersed in the data.

"Yes. Death Valley. Class seven terrain. It hasn't been ground-searched for good reason..." He keyed in the toxicity readings. "Recent earthquake and continuing volcanic activity along with its normally severe climate have rendered it uninhabitable, unstable, and off-limits to surface surveillance."

"Exactly, Lucan. For that reason I want an on-the-ground search."

Why waste men and materiél exploring this ring of hell? Desmond thought in exasperation. "Sir, it's inhumanly hot. The temperature today was—" He consulted a graph, "—one hundred and twenty-two degrees. There's no water beyond minor surface collection, ground troops are limited to light vehicles and small side arms. The land is highly unstable, use of any major firepower risks a chain reaction and atmospheric contam—"

"Yes, I realize that as well. But theoretically, weapons will be unnecessary for anything but defense against indigenous animal life, which is likely to be reptilian. Still, I understand your objections, Lucan. Make it a job for volunteers fully equipped with protective gear. Offer a bonus."

"Yes, sir. But I don't see how these women could possibly..."

He trailed off as the Premier looked at him sagely. "Do you really put anything past them, Lucan?"

Desmond met his gaze in perfect understanding. "No, sir, I don't," he said softly.

He addressed Kenan Vartan. "General, get a volunteer detachment ready and a plan of action to carry out the Premier's orders. Canvass this Death Valley area. Thoroughly."

"It's done," Vartan said, opening his communicator.

2201.10.03—AFRICA

The desert that surrounds us is vast, silent, intimidating; profoundly and achingly empty. At dusk, Joss and I are invisible specks in our sand-colored cloaks, on a landscape cooling from a day of burning white-blue sky and stark, pitiless clarity. The land, washed and bleached by blasting sun, is glazed with the violet, ocher, and amber colors of evening.

This land, where Mother Earth is least bountiful, least forgiving, has always ignited in me metaphorical imagery—the biblical mythology of isolation and ordeal. This land has also always been a prime exemplar that civilization, no matter its comfort and safety, its inventions and technology, is a thin veneer that can be and is in fact being stripped away, and Theo Zedera is far from the only cause. Desert encroaches everywhere: Environmental depredation and global warming, beginning with the excesses of the twentieth and twenty-first centuries, have increased its area from one-fifth to one-third of global land mass, and fresh water shortages become ever more critical...

Joss has been silent. She too has been affected by the austere grandeur of our surroundings. I realize, also, that besides protection of me another reason for her to be here is that she views mutinously our living circumstances—this last confided to me recently by Olympia. Enmeshed as I am in every detail of building and securing our world, I do not share Joss's feeling of imprisonment, but I do identify with her yearning to escape it and to be here on the surface however inimical it may be, and for however brief a time; no one who chose to remain on Earth bargained for this open-ended exile. We assumed reentry at some point into a free and unhidden, if clandestine, society of our own choice and devising. That we are in these circumstances…

Forcing my thoughts away from this all too familiar track that leads to Theo Zedera, I focus on what remains to be done of our work. We have been fully occupied in running tests all day, and Joss and I have signaled enough adjustments to our holography to amply justify my insistence on making this journey to the surface. Sunset will change the perceptions of anyone venturing on this land; thus one final twilight check must be completed before we journey by flight pak back to our entry tunnel. While I await new images and adjusted settings from our team, I take in my surroundings, and my young companion.

All the women in our Unity are beautiful. But this young woman, with her strong body and supple athleticism, her clear eyes the color of the subtly darkening sky behind her, and a fresh, sweet face with life's experience only beginning its imprint, would be a distraction to anyone.

When she looks up from her recorder and meets my gaze, for a brief, mesmerizing moment a heat rises in me, unconnected to the burning desert. Somewhere amid the keenness of recognizing desires that I no longer countenance, that I thought I had put away forever, I understand that she is far more of a distraction than I can possibly afford. For the sake of us both I must keep my wits about me. Now, and in the future.

"This is among the most distinctive places on Earth," I

remark as I pull my gaze away from her. I suspect she has resisted searching out any of the readily available facts about this valley she so resents, but wonder if anything impacted her when Viridia and Rozene conducted their briefings. "Would you agree?"

"I agree, it's amazing." Her voice is husky, subdued, her tone ambiguous. "Every geological era is represented here."

Shifting my desert pak, I bend to scoop up a handful of stones. "And nearly every kind, color, and hardness of rock." I extract a small black rock from my handful. "Once molten lava, and not all that long ago." I let the stones sift back down to the desert floor and gesture to the distant, deeply folded hills. "Metamorphic rock more than a billion years old—Precambrian through Cenozoic, all the great eras of geologic time, deformed by folding and faulting. Yet the Lyon-Martin Range, the Stein-Toklas—all the major mountain ranges around us—emerged only recently, the last four or five million years. This place is wondrous. Magnificent."

She is looking around, following my gesture, but as the wind comes up in a lonely sigh, wisps of sand begin to blow across our boots and anxiety floods her face. I suddenly feel it too. This wind is gentle, nonthreatening, and utterly deceptive: Wind in actuality is the most powerful force in the desert. And there is something else out there besides wind.

Call it intuition. Even though I too have been eager to be out here on the surface, I feel my skin prickling, I sense what Joss senses. Danger lurks, somewhere near us.

Shadows fall over the land. Moving. Several birds with heavy, sharp-hooked beaks and broad wings with deeply feathered tips have soared into view, aloft on the hot evening winds in slow, wide spirals. Vultures. But along with death, life, stubborn life, abounds in this poisoned place, multitudes of insects, the lizards, scorpions, rats, and rabbits found in every desert, burros and coyotes, squirrels and kit foxes. They are mostly nocturnal; Joss and I have seen none of them except a few rabbits and reptiles. We have seen faint animal tracks, and occasionally parallel lines a meter or so in length and several centimeters apart—the signature of the sidewinder, one of many species of rattlesnake, the most evolutionarily advanced denizen of this desert and its deadliest predator. After dark it will hunt with radar-like, heat-seeking precision.

Plants have seized their place here through marvels of adaptation—not just cactus, the classic desert native, but the desert holly that thrives on salt and dryness, and sagebrush with its distasteful sap, protection against insects. And creosote bush conversely supports a coterie of insects that will live nowhere else.

"It once rained here," Joss remarks, shifting her desert pak to gesture to one of the gravel fans formed over the centuries from debris washing down from the mountains. The fan is coated with desert varnish, a dark layer of iron and manganese oxides. "I miss rain..." Her tone is mournful.

I nod. I miss it too. "Rozene told me that in most places half the rainfall normally evaporates into the atmosphere. Here, it's ninety percent—no surprise when temperatures are like today." I consult my wrist pak. "A hundred and thirty degrees out on the salt pan."

"We don't belong here," she says. "And that's not just my own stubbornness. We've never belonged in any of the deserts. The one species least well adapted to desert is our own."

I search for an argument but have to concede, "You're right. From the standpoint that technology, surely not physiology, allows us to be here. Daria tells me that without properly insulated clothing like ours, we could perspire nearly twenty pints in a day—no amount of drinking water could replace it. Without protection we'd dehydrate at the rate of five percent of body weight a day."

"It's a harsh, cruel place."

"A challenging place, even an inspirational place," I reply.

I've heard that the desert is capable of inspiring a kind of epiphany, an almost physical sense of liberation of mind and spirit. This desert has, this very moment, succeeded in kindling something like that in me. I tell Joss, "This defiled but defiant desert is an object lesson in evolution, adaptation..."

As I search my mind for more facts, I realize that this is the one area in which I have only the most general knowledge, and most of that was imparted to me by Theo Zedera. Sociology, genetics, evolution, adaptation—these were Theo's areas of expertise...never mine...

"Mayday. Mayday. Mayday."

Quietly voiced. Simultaneous on my wrist pak and Joss's.

We have been too rigorously trained and rehearsed by Vellmar to question this command for one instant. I follow the first rule of procedure: Do not look for the danger, simply respond. Fling off your cloak, grasp it by the collar, activate the pin imbedded under the collar.

Joss has followed the same instructions in exact choreography with me, except she has leaped the few meters between us and seized me. In milliseconds both our cloaks have ballooned over and around us, inflating to many times their size.

In the aftermath of our instinctive reaction to the emergency signal, our haste to secure our safety, we look to each other in the half-light. The adrenaline rush reflected in Joss's heaving chest and glittering eyes is, I'm sure, apparent in me as well. I place a finger over my lips and she nods. Our wrist paks automatically deactivated after the Mayday call and will not return to life until and unless the danger passes; we cannot, must not speak. Whatever the nature of this emergency, we dare not create the slightest sound wave detectable by instrumentation. I, better than anyone, know about surveillance instruments that will pick up as anomalous the most tenuous of sounds.

We are enveloped in a dusky world, its porous outer circumference allowing the entry of breathable air; but it will deflect anything save water—although we would surely not drown in this desert climate—and laser fire, which no sane individual would unleash here, not where a chain reaction of incalculable destructiveness would ensue.

Our ingenious protective "bubble" is one of the defensive strategies perfected by nanotechnologist Vellmar over the months when we were effectuating the escape of our other sisters. Chameleon-like in its chemistry, when deployed it morphs into the colors and appearance of the land it occupies; it now appears identical to the sandblasted rock and the naturally occurring feldspar on this ancient landscape. To alleviate what would otherwise be tomb-like blackness, Vellmar designed it to absorb and store sun and moonlight through its Fluxbar coating that defeats probing; so our interior is illuminated, but calibrated so as to be a natural part of the landscape to any onlooker even in the dark of night.

We are neither blind nor deaf in this rock igloo; we have aural and optic devices that appear to be innocuous dark spots on our rock's rugged exterior. And so we virtually bump heads in our haste to survey our surroundings.

The cause of the emergency signal is immediately apparent, and after a single glance Joss backs away, fear etched on her face. She is a strong young woman, but she has never been in a situation of physical jeopardy. I, of course, do what a synthesist does: assess what confronts us. In this case, a military force rapidly emerging into view, darkening the horizon as it approaches, dwarfed by its own column of dust as it floats just above the sands and gravel of our rocky desert in black, fully armored ATVs. Obviously our Sisterhood's scanning devices picked them up as soon as they broke this northern perimeter of Sappho Valley, and, judging by their speed of approach, it appears that our instant response to the Mayday call has saved us; a few more seconds and their forward observer scanners would have spotlighted our body mass, would have recorded us inflating our cloaks. There would have been no possibility of escape and a prime means of self-defense for our Sisterhood would have been rendered useless. But the true calamity would have been our capture...

Surreptitiously, I brush a wave of gooseflesh from my arms, then occupy my mind with observations.

I estimate their ranks at several thousand, and a formidable sight they are in their silvery protective gear and face masks, their uniforms designed to deflect field weapon fire or chemical assault, their masks to filter out toxins. Obviously they travel here in full realization of the dangers. Their vehicles, although bristling with gear, display no heavy weaponry.

Without question this is a reconnaissance party, ultimate proof of what I have always contended to my sisters: More than two years after our disappearance Zed's search for us remains obsessive. All our subterfuge, all the impediments we have created, will not deflect his determination to scour every inch of this planet for us. I can only wonder if this is a full-scale operation—whether other incursions have been made at the same time as this one into Sappho Valley. We have wide-view sensors installed on Faderman's View, Grahn Point, and Djuna Pass to guard our eastern flank. Our southern sentinel is Radclyffe Pass, with Lorde Butte and Allison Peak on our western perimeter. This particular invasion has entered via the northern route, Rule Canyon. Have our early warning monitors been sufficient to meet the challenge? This first test of our defenses may well not be the last, and outwitting these highly resourceful predators without rousing their suspicion will be vital in determining the frequency and sophistication of their searches of our valley.

Joss and I can do nothing but wait. Until the contingent passes us, until it completes its sweep of the area, until our sisters activate our wrist paks and send the all-clear signal.

My anguish and frustration at being trapped here are inexpressible. This feels like no less than another failure. Now, when the need is most imperative, I am part of the problem. Not only will I not be where my talents would be most useful—assisting my sisters in their defensive assessments and maneuvers—I will be siphoning off their attention as they closely monitor our situation.

My sole consolation is that our preparations have been thorough. Every contingency we could conceive of has been covered, and Tara will be exercising her considerable leadership and decision-making skills as surveillance data pours in. Protection screens will have been lowered by now on Tiptree Forest and on our hydroponic units, all but the most basic survival systems shut down everywhere. My sisters will merely observe the enemy and wait quietly as Joss and I wait, either for their departure or for any aggressive act that will force countermeasures.

I know full well that our most dangerous enemy is the unexpected, which waits, as it always does, in ambush.

The desert, with its punishing heat and cold, its abrading winds, is an entity unto itself that for eons has scoured away evidence of the presence of human beings. We must rely on it now to be our harsh ally. Will these men find what we want them to find—only a barren, inimical landscape? Barren...which is not to say lifeless... And by its nature a threat to them despite all their armor.

Joss gathers herself and steps up to have another look, then gestures urgently to me.

My consternation matches hers. They are not passing us. Instead they are landing their vehicles in a tight circle and are unloading equipment in the choreographed moves of well-trained soldiers in the process of bivouacking for the night. Or perhaps longer.

Joss circles an arm about my shoulders then jerks away in consternation at her involuntary act, but I draw her back to me. We must remain calm and quiet. We are safe here—provided we remain a part of the terrain like the desert sagebrush that tumbles past us in the gusting winds of evening.

I take inventory of the situation. Our habitat is small but not oppressively so, thanks to the simultaneous deployment of our cloaks. We can stand, and lie down fully stretched out. With our desert paks we are provisioned with energy tabs and the standard supply of three days' water, which can be easily stretched to four or more if need be. Our one-piece bacteria-infused clothing is thoroughly self-cleaning, versatile, climate-controlled, and will decompose all bodily waste to its elements as if we were still moving over the desert surface.

Amid the commotion of the soldiers establishing camp around us, it is safe to secure our own quarters; for the moment we need not be concerned with attracting attention to our own activity. On my signal Joss and I release the tab on our sleeping mats; like oil they spread over the stony floor of our chamber to provide comfort for sitting—and sleeping, if such an act could be possible in these circumstances. We are insulated both from the sun and the cold desert night. Physically, we will be comfortable enough. Considering that we sit virtually in the camp of the enemy.

My skin crawls as I look at the soldiers around us. I feel Theo Zedera close to me, as if somehow, in some way, he senses that I am here. It is surely I who have drawn him here...

This incursion is, in a way, as necessary to us as it is to him. That it had to happen I have always known as certainty. We have lived in continuous tension with the knowledge. Now that the test is here, my sisters will meet it with all the strategies we have devised, and beyond that, with courage and resourcefulness.

If all goes according to plan, the henchmen of Theo Zedera will come and go like a forest fire sweeping over us. My focus now must be to prevent my own fear from paralyzing me, to look after Joss and keep my promise to Tara to return her safely.

2201.10.04—JOSS

Nighttime in the camp of the invader. Deep night. But not dark enough night. The camp perimeter is lit with narrow strips of brilliance that Africa says will immobilize and disintegrate anything that ventures near them. I hear the *zzzzzt* sounds that confirm what she says: innocent desert creatures drawn to the light and to annihilation.

This night's events began at sundown with the security sweep of the campsite, during which Africa and I watched and waited in absolute stillness. I could scarcely breathe during the *tock tock tock* of the instruments that slowly, methodically swept and analyzed our rock, rigid with anxiety that Vellmar's creation would not pass muster and that they would detect through our Fluxbar protection a pounding of my heart that hurt my chest with its violence. Then came these constant, sickening *zzzzzt* killing sounds. And the sentries, about a dozen I could see in our part of the encampment—who knows how many others—changing guard duty every hour, marching in close formation and then dispersing to stand twenty paces apart in those slick silver uniforms, faces hidden behind black visors, legs braced apart, a hand on the barrel of a rifle, the butt end resting on the desert floor.

It was three or four hours ago, as nearly as I can reckon

time with all our instrumentation shut down, that my whole being was wrapped entirely in a longing to be working side by side with my sisters on our defense operations. Vowing that if I ever got back there, if I got out of this alive, I'd never again protest having to live in Sappho Valley. Our bubble, so dark and claustrophobic, its air warm and thick and close, is only a shade or two removed from pitch-blackness, and this danger all around us makes our other underground home seem a paradise.

Even after the security sweep, when we were no longer in immediate peril, the aftermath of my adrenaline surge made it impossible for me to sit still. It was at this point that I turned away from staring out of an optiscan to sit beside Africa with a whispered question: "Why these sentries? You told me their scanners picked up everything."

"They do," she murmured in reply. "For miles. Everything larger than a mouse. The sentries are useless." Her voice seemed calm, as did her demeanor; but she was barely discernible in the darkness, her slender form a still, ebony shadow.

She had been occasionally rising to perform a survey of our situation, telling me each time there was no real information to be gleaned till morning, and of course she was right, but sleep clearly was not a possibility for either of us, so every few minutes I yielded to my compulsion to leap up and look out, while she sat cross-legged, hands on her knees as if in meditation.

She said to me, "This fact is obscured in historical records, but we briefly had female combat soldiers around the twenty-first century."

I could only utter in incredulity, "We *did*?"

"We did. Inevitably they began to question military traditions, to establish proof that posturing of this kind," her gesture took in the sentries, "added nothing to any nation's defense and actually incited and prolonged hostilities. Which was widely interpreted as proof that we lacked the aptitude and the heart for military service. We haven't been allowed into anything but minor support roles ever since."

"Soldiers?" I was confounded. "We wanted to be soldiers? To kill people? Why?"

"As part of the struggle for equality with men in times past. An endless and fruitless struggle, as you know. Our true nature won out," she added, and I thought I saw her lips curve into a slight smile. "The point is, those sentries out there don't have a purpose, logical or military, except as an exhibition of chest beating, the continuing mythology of the warrior as hero. Mythology that's been celebrated down through the ages from the ancient times of Homer. Military mentality has never changed, has always lagged behind the weapons invented for war, a lag we can now measure in centuries. Which is why war is so increasingly barbaric—why we've gone from killing thousands to the slaughter of hundreds of millions."

The pervasive, formidable hum from all the monitoring and communication equipment around us gave testament to her assessment. I stared at her in fascination, straining to see something of her face in the darkness. Even though synthesizing a myriad of facts is her profession, how in these circumstances could she be as calmly analytical as she sounded? Then the truth penetrated my thick skull: She wasn't.

The vulnerability she must feel—compared to her, I should be as serene as a pond in winter. Where was my strength, this strength of mine in which I had always such taken pride, that I had yearned to place in the service of this irreplaceable woman?

Of any of us in the Unity, her capture would be by far the most catastrophic. If I were taken, I would be nothing to them—a nothing they'd drug, question, and disintegrate when they were finished. But Africa—Africa they would take directly to Zed, and killing her would be the last and least thing he'd do to her. How he would make use of such a trophy before a worldwide public was simply beyond imagination, and my mind shrank from it.

Impaled with grief over her peril, a peril that seemingly would never end in a world that had become a cauldron of unmitigated savagery, I reached to her, touched her face. And recoiled—the warmth of her skin jolting me into realization of what I had done, however involuntary, however well meaning. The second involuntary act of this night—I had previously placed an arm around her shoulders. My blundering, my temerity—the boldness of my impulse to touch her—were inexcusable .

"A—Africa, I—"

Amid this stammering attempt at an apology, a miracle occurred.

She took my clenched, offending hand. Brought it back to her. Opened it and pressed my palm into the smooth soft skin of her cheek. Then eased my hand away from her face to hold it for a moment as if gauging its weight; and brought it to her lap and held it between her hands.

My hand warmed between her two; and I felt my body warming as well, as if it—as if all of my self—were being held between those gentle hands. She traced each finger with the feathery touch of her fingertips, as if wanting to learn only their shape. Then, knitting her fingers into my own, she brought my hand back to her face. To her lips...

The sweet softness of her lips, her breath caressing my fingers—it was so quickly unbearable that I had to withdraw my hand as if from fire. Only to reach for her again, a compulsion. This time not simply to touch her face, but to have the substance of her.

Holding her. In the opaque depths of this terrifying place enfolding the slenderness of her...I felt a rigidity in her that I would have known as resistance had it not had in it a quivering, so very slight it could have originated deep within the earth to emerge through her. I tightened my arms and felt some of her tension ease, and with a sigh breathed against my ear she slid her hands, her arms up my back and clasped my shoulders. My face resting tenderly against hers, I held her, aware only of her body slowly, slowly softening as the tremors diminished...

A sob. A convulsion, huge, gulping, seeming as if it too, like her trembling, had vented from out of the earth itself. Her entire body engulfed in spasms of sobbing, she smothered her face in my shoulder, burying her cries, whether from me or from those around us, I did not know. But I softly told her, "Cry. Just cry..."

I knew there were no sentries near us. Their closest shelter, a camouflaged pod, was perhaps a hundred yards away. The surveillance systems appeared to be directed outward now that the camp itself had been thoroughly swept. While I did not think anyone could hear Africa under these circumstances and amid all the background sounds in this military bivouac, it was still a hopeful guess. But as she cried in my arms I realized she had judged us safe because from what I now knew of her, she cared nothing of herself but would protect me at all costs. I held her closely, perfectly willing to hold her till morning.

Some time much later: "Thank you," she murmured, and her lips touched mine, a whisper-light briefness.

Just as lightly, just as briefly, I kissed her back—to simply say to her how willing I was to be the someone in whose arms she could hide, to whom she could cling while her anguish poured from her.

Her hands cradled my face. Her fingers twined in my

hair. And in this dark and deadly dangerous place I drew her to me again. And our lips met again, softly, so gently, she seeking the shape of my lips as I did hers, her delicate, soft lips.

Her lips glided over my cheek, my eyelid, my temple; her warm breath bathed my ear. "Joss," she exhaled.

"Yes," I whispered. And in my utterance of the word was my yes to everything, to anything.

Her arms sliding around my shoulders, a hand delicate on the back of my neck...her lips came to mine, pressed so sweetly into mine. Began to part under mine...and then pulled abruptly away.

"I have no right..." She gasped for breath, her body surging, and I held her, my face in her hair, held her as her body convulsed again and again with sobs, her hands fluttering on my back.

For a timeless while I held her. Kissed her face. Tasting the salt on her wet cheeks, in her tear-filled eyes. I lowered her to spread my body over her. To be her barrier, her bulwark, a protection against the entire universe. Her shell. Within that, to provide comfort from her grief.

"This horror...all of it...all my fault," she wept.

"You didn't do this," I breathed, my lips touching her ear. "Any of it."

"I could have stopped it before it began." Seizing my shoulders, she added in an almost inaudible whisper, "That you're here with me now—it's all my fault."

I could not tell her how gratified I was to be with her, how willingly I would be with her anywhere, even inside this gate to hell. I could not tell her how I loved her, how I had always loved her. To say any of these things, to say I had worshiped her all my life would prejudice in her eyes anything I said, would challenge any claim I had to judgment. "It's not your fault," I said.

"You don't understand," she said in a fierce whisper. "You don't know."

"I do understand," I insisted, and held her face between my hands, straining without avail to see beyond the opaque shadow of her face into her eyes. "I do know. You did none of this. None of it. You set none of it in motion."

"Had I known what he was—"

"Had you known, then yes, you could hold yourself to blame."

"Joss..." The next words were a hiss: *"I should have known."*

"But you didn't. And if you didn't, no one could have."

"You don't understand," she said in despair. "No one could have known him as I did. I knew him like my own soul. I should have—"

"Listen to me." I gripped her shoulders. "You may never understand why you didn't see this. No one ever knows anyone in every way. Unless you *are* that other person. My mother was stunned that I didn't go with her and my sisters to the stars. So even mothers don't know their own children like that."

She was quiet, then said, "How have you come by such wisdom, Joss?" With a hint of lightness in her tone, even though her question was posed with the utmost seriousness.

From loving you, I answered within me, knowing I could not voice it. I asked instead, "Do you believe me, Africa?"

Again she was silent, this time for a long while, her hand stroking the hair at the back of my neck while she considered my question. Then: "For this night I believe you."

It was more than I had expected. Ever.

"You're very strong," she whispered, her hands clasping, exploring my shoulders. "In many ways."

"Only in some ways," I murmured in return.

"Stronger than you know."

The truth was, I was far, far weaker than she knew. Especially as her lips brushed my face. And I became weaker still when she pressed the unfasten tabs on her clothes, then my own; and when she drew me down with her onto our cushioned floor I dissolved, body, mind and heart, into the warm silky softness of her.

I hardly dared to caress the soft warm flesh so open to my hands, but soon it did not matter. She was the one who fit us together, so that our entire bodies were a mutual caressing. When her lips opened under mine to take my tongue inside her, when her legs opened to hold me between them, ours was a fusion so intimate that I felt her pleasure within me with each movement of my body on hers.

In pleasure that was excruciating I felt everything. The tension in her hands and the fingers spread over my back, the straining in the muscles of the thighs of the legs wrapped around me, the frenzy of her tongue against mine, her gasps for breath against my ear when she had to take her mouth from mine as I moved on her, the writhing of her hips as I matched her rhythms. Like the music I create I drew from her melody to my harmony. Enhancing, prolonging the sweetest heights of the melody, varying the melody...repeating, repeating...

She did not need my fingers or tongue for any of her orgasms, but I did taste her, drink from her, an indulgence since she clearly only wanted my body in her arms, but I held her quivering thighs against my heated face until she gasped her need. Then I laid my body on hers again, fused with the writhing of her hips and her final paroxysms, my body vibrating with her orgasm.

She sleeps now, in a graceful curl. In so deep a sleep that I clothed her without her awakening, and myself as well, even though I would dearly love to gaze at her body in its lovely brown nakedness as dawn enters our valley. But night has brought a coldness that seeped into our shelter, a coldness we did not feel in the heat of our coupling.

In these first gray hints of dawn I will say this: If I live out this day, no matter what befalls me in the rest of my life the memory of this night will sustain me for the rest of my days, however many or few they may be.

2201.10.04—OLYMPIA

In the history of our Unity, these are the five days that hold the most significance: Day One, the beginning of it all, Mother gives birth to the original nine of our Unity. Day Two, all of us abdicate our involvement in the affairs of Earth. Day Three, our sisters leave for the stars to create their own world. Day Four, those of us remaining behind choose our new home. And now, as the first hints of predawn faintly lighten Sappho Valley, there is this Day Five, the one for which we have so assiduously prepared, and, speaking for myself, so dreaded: the day we must protect and defend our home.

Since the invasion last night and our Mayday call to Africa and Joss, our entire Unity has been assembled in our amphitheater deep underground, the Fluxbar-coated chamber we finished constructing only a year ago for this express emergency. All other areas of our evacuated abode have been left in defense-readiness. We have an exit pathway leading to the surface miles outside the western perimeter of our valley, traversable by gopher cart but artfully constructed to resemble declivities and irregularities within Mother Earth herself.

It does not escape me, our Unity's historian, that if our home is destroyed and this pathway is blocked or demolished we will take our place among those other misty legends, the lost island of Atlantis, the Amazons of Scythia, the goddess culture—history that inconveniently contravenes the records the chroniclers would have the world accept. If we die down here our bones will never be found and our adversaries will erase us from recorded history, our existence consigned to rumor and conjecture just like all those other societies.

Some of us still doze fitfully; others watch the multitude of data receptors that monitor and analyze activity in the encampment surrounding Africa and Joss, and in the second camp of invaders on our eastern flank. All our children under the age of ten sleep in a side chamber, away from this main center of activity. When they awaken they will have their usual classes and entertainments. They have been made aware of the invasion by our psychologist, Helene, who told them the basic facts in her easy, composed fashion, and assured them of their safety. They sleep calmly, understanding that although they will be away from this center of activity they will be kept informed of events, along with the teachers and caregivers who remain with them. We previously discussed allowing them into this amphitheater to be with the rest of us, and arrived at a consensus that we would not risk traumatizing them with actual views of the invaders on our valley floor. Our first sighting of the black-clad army of Zed and its weapons and bristling array of armored vehicles has confirmed the wisdom of that decision.

We have the hideaway of Africa and Joss in our sights and closely track all activity around them. They of course know that like the two of them, we can only sit and watch and wait. We cannot act until our invaders act.

Africa and Joss cannot know about the second invasion that followed the one into Rule Canyon, although Africa will surely surmise this may have happened. The other encampment, under Faderman's View, would be within sight of Tiptree Forest had we not shuttered it into a self-sustaining giant terrarium until our return. Better we cannot see the invaders' camp from there, because its malignant presence in that spectacular place in our valley and within view of our beloved forest seems especially a defilement. It is the unspoken, desperate hope of all of us that Tiptree Forest will survive, that destruction of this indescribably precious treasure will not end up a defensive necessity.

Our huge chamber is a colorful if sobering scene. From floor to ceiling, women occupy niches hollowed out of our rock walls, and they follow and participate in these proceedings on their personal communicators. Their faces differ, representing all the peoples of Earth in beautiful racial mixtures, but now they hold a single expression in common: worry. Our animal companions are with us, and we give them the stroking comfort we yearn for ourselves.

In the center of us all is Tara, who is sitting up now on her sleeping mat, smoothing her pants and shirt, shaking her hair, and combing blond strands away from her face with her fingers. As she looks around at us, then assesses the activity at the monitors, I see an intensification of anticipation and even excitement in her gray eyes at what this day will bring.

Our leader leaps lightly to her feet, strides over to pick up a container of the hot tea Wilda has provided, and looks as fresh and energized as if she had slept through the night. She did sleep some of the time, in demonstration of her confidence that we are as prepared as we can be, and that our invaders, despite their incursion at dusk, had no rationale to act under cover of darkness and would wait till morning. An opinion not fully shared by some of us, including myself. Unable to take my eyes from the monitors and data ports, I have not slept this night, nor has my sister, who sits at the center consoles along with the equally sleepless Rakel, Rozene, Viridia, and Raina, our strategic team who endlessly run preparedness checks on our defense grid.

Our only operating systems on or anywhere near the surface are devoted solely to defense, solar-powered to emit no trace evidence of their existence. Our imaging and projection network has been activated to pick up motion-generated images from anywhere on our valley surface via hillside sensors and projectors no more visible than grains of sand. Our invaders are fully in view—they will make no move without us observing them. Thanks to the verifications run by Africa and Joss, we have a greater degree of certitude that our holography is in optimum readiness for implementation.

There are unknown factors, of course. Whether there will be additional incursions in support of these two. How far toward Bannon Crater they plan to penetrate. Most importantly, how quickly this invading force can be convinced that no human life exists in our valley. The longer they stay, the greater our jeopardy. There's also the possibility that despite all our contingency planning, our invaders may bring to bear on us weapons or search devices unknown to us...

As dawn nears, the Rule Canyon camp of the invaders comes to life, and it is an odd sensation to know that Africa sees what we see. I cannot help wondering what she has experienced this night with young Joss in her care.

A collective gasp of horror from our entire Unity. Tara, in the process of lifting her tea to her lips, freezes mid-motion.

In the dusty, wind-filled dawn, six soldiers approach the hideaway of Africa and Joss. Their direction unmistakable, their advance a purposeful march. The hair rises on the back of my neck.

They halt at the rock. Reach to their belts. How have they managed to discover—

The soldiers have come over for a definite purpose indeed. As they urinate all over the rocklike shell holding our two sisters, our laughter is loud and raucous with relief. Imagining how discomfited Africa and Joss must be at this act and our witnessing of it, we become almost hysterical.

We soon sober, however, as other images crowd our monitors, views from both camps of soldiers exiting their pods, breaking out mess kits, readying equipment and vehicles, checking their weapons. Edges of their uniforms flutter and flap in rising winds, gusts blowing dust and sand around their boots.

Tara sits before a large grid pattern of immense complexity, the schematic of our valley. "Rozene?" she asks softly of our climate specialist.

"Winds of fifteen to twenty, Tara, gusting to forty-five," replies Rozene.

"And forty-five carries up to nine times as much sand as fifteen-mile-an-hour winds," Tara says, as if reminding herself of this formula.

"Correct."

"Excellent. Stand by."

I know full well that Tara feels keenly the jeopardy to Africa and Joss. Yet she operates from one stance only: This is a situation we can and will rectify. The room around us has become vibrant with voices and activity as everyone sees to her assigned task, and this is Tara's doing; she has projected onto our Unity her purpose and energy. We are braced, we are ready to play our roles of defender to the extent of our abilities, whether that be as data monitor, food provider, child-care giver, activities coordinator. All of us will be all of these things, depending on how long the invaders remain in our valley.

As a sandstorm sweeps the valley, increasing in force, the Faderman's View camp continues with its preparations, but the Rule Canyon invaders have erased their protective perimeter force field and are preparing to break camp. "Bannon Crater," Tara says.

"Magma feed complete. Fusion fuses ignited. Temperature elevation of point seven-two-three-five degrees. As scheduled," Viridia reports. Her voice is calm but her face is austere in its focus and determination.

"Perfect," murmurs Tara.

"Sunrise forty seconds," Willa calls.

"Ready holography," Tara says.

"Ready," Raina says softly, a hand poised over her console.

"Program one, program five."

Shouts and much commotion from both Rule Canyon and Faderman's View as dawn breaks over our valley.

As the ground bucks under their feet, forces in both camps halt all activity, frozen in astonishment in the pink-gray light. They mill about in confusion at the sight of the towering steam cloud from Bannon Crater.

In the rising winds of Rule Canyon a burly and heavily muscled commander, clearly fearless with his physical gifts, is pulling off his helmet as if he needs to view the scene with his vision unadulterated by a visor. Just as clearly, he is stupid. His blond hair whipping violently in the sand-laden winds, he momentarily squints into the desert landscape, then falls to his knees, clawing at his eyes, desperately fumbling his helmet back over skin that in those few exposed seconds has been flayed by sandblasting.

Sand streams across a desert floor that oozes, teems, abounds, is overrun with reptiles. As far as the eye can see—a distance rapidly diminishing—is a writhing mass of sidewinders, diamondback rattlers, banded geckos, iguanas, collared lizards, leopard lizards, zebra-tailed lizards, horned and striped lizards. Lizards darting, slithering. Snakes coiling, uncoiling, writhing, striking at bodies around them.

Another commander, this one presumably with more than half of his wits about him, is forcefully gesticulating as he gives orders over his helmet communicator. The stunned soldiers obey as best they can in the howling, screaming wind, some struggling into ATVs, others moving into disciplined formation ten abreast behind the windbreaking protection of the force fields being erected around their vehicles. Then, led by their slowly advancing ATVs, they move forward in the dawn light of a desert drowning under the blowing sand.

"Winds at forty-five," Rozene reports. "Gusts to sixty-five."

Those sixty-five-mile-an-hour gusts scream across the land, blowing sand horizontally, visibility lowering by the moment. The reptiles writhe, scarcely evading the effortful strides of the soldiers. A commander's head jerks as he barks a command. The soldiers ready their weapons.

"Ready nine, sixteen, twelve," Tara orders.

Weapon fire erupts on the desert floor.

"Now," Tara orders.

Visibility approaches zero as the bodies of creatures fly in the dust and sand, chunks of body parts landing in a splattering, oozing of fluid.

The soldiers advance no further. In a somewhat orderly formation they retreat. Climb into vehicles which lift above the desert floor, then immediately land: There is no vertical escape from this sandstorm. They put up their protective fields to deflect the force and effect of the storm while they wait. They can go nowhere.

If they have geologists with them, and surely they do

for terrain like this, then they have already noted the presence of ventifacts—boulders sculpted and deeply abraded by sandblasting—all over this landscape in testimony to the destructive power of sand carried by wind. What is happening now should not seem unusual. Nor should the extreme profusion of reptilian life if the toxicity of this land, and the absence of human life for nearly forty years, are taken into the equation.

In the other camp, the one under Faderman's View, winds are not so fierce, because of the configuration of the terrain, but they are nevertheless increasing in velocity and laden with sand. This camp has moved its vehicles into airborne position, and they are sending thin electronic sensor probes deep into the Earth, in horizontal and vertical paths.

This is grievous to us. Every piercing of the earth anywhere near our abode triggers a cave-in. A cave-in planned in advance of the probe, designed so that the probe will find only the composite rock it is supposed to find, and no evidence of the chambers and tunnels—the home we have constructed.

I watch all this in fascination and dread and anguish, scarcely able to perform my duties as historian. As the winds pick up below Faderman's View, the probing vehicles cease their operations and they too settle back onto the desert floor and erect their own force fields, defeated by sand and wind.

We have brought this invading army to a standstill.

For the moment, only for the moment, we are victorious.

This is what we have done, as I understand it. On the glassine surfaces of our desert where silica combines with lime and soda, when denizens like snakes or reptiles happen to slither onto it they lose the normal traction that allows them their usual graceful and efficient, if languid, movements on normal sand. They also lose their torpor as they struggle mightily to escape a surface where any movement is suddenly effortful and uncontrollable. This struggle, this writhing—these were the images we recorded and enhanced, these were the images from which we created our holograms. Permanent holograms projected onto the desert floor. Or as permanent as we wish them to be.

I do not view these images willingly, and if forced to do so, revulsion all but wrenches out my intestines. It is no consolation that humans are universally repulsed, if not terrified, by reptilian life even though such creatures are connected with our own origins, our emergence from the seas. Could it be, it occurs to me, that our revulsion is for this very reason? That we view reptiles in the same manner and for the same reason as afterbirth? The reptiles in our desert in their natural state would give pause to even the most stouthearted. We have enhanced their size in our holograms. Anyone venturing into our valley will find areas of its floor covered with a writhing mass of oversize reptiles, and will know that they cannot be destroyed by the usual method of laying down laser fire. Any invader must use far lesser weapons. And since we know what they must use, and the effects of those weapons, we have created another series of holograms, these providing vivid evidence of the even more revolting "results" of the "carnage"—contorting, slimy reptilian body parts.

In the rare times when holography has been implemented as a device in warfare or as a defensive measure in war, it has served to exaggerate the number of actual troops and weaponry. Africa has told me that theories abound for its other uses but have always been rejected no matter how compellingly the arguments are made for the potential to lessen the devastation of war. Employing trickery and subterfuge as part of a nation's war defenses is deemed psychologically damaging to the fighting troops who dismiss such methods as cowardly at their base. The prevailing line of thinking, apparently, is that if hostilities between two or more groups come to the boiling point of war, then battles must be fought and won or lost; there must be tangible slaughter, a visible and memorable result. We in our Unity see no redemptive value in this abhorrent justification for savagery and carnage and inhuman conduct.

As to the storm that rages on our valley floor, our winds occur naturally and constantly, the Sierra Nevada mountain range an impervious boundary keeping rain bottled on its western side, while our desert winds slam into its eastern flank. By creating additional lava flow, by adjusting temperature gradients at Bannon Crater to suddenly heat our landscape and radically affect wind movement we can, however, enhance our winds if need be, and to near-lethal levels.

These are the primary defense "weapons" we have now shown to our invaders, along with the historically legendary heat of the place, Mother Earth's own method of discouraging human presence, as if she would keep this part of herself to herself. We hold in abeyance floods of contaminated water that will thunder down washes when this expeditionary force comes anywhere near them. We have holographic insects that we cannot employ in these winds, but if the combatants remain through more clement conditions, vast swarms will hover over their camps, their equipment, their bodies. We also have a capability we will not use: a pyroclastic flow from our volcano that would destroy them entirely...

Our invaders have hunkered down and will not leave our desert while our winds scream through the canyons. They may then run more of their tests and complete what they consider a thorough search routine. We have done our best, have a few more tricks up our sleeve, and as nearly as I can see it has all been accomplished flawlessly thus far. If I were a soldier in their camp, if I were a commander under these horrific climatic conditions, I know exactly what I would put in my report: *No evidence of human life, or that human life could exist above or below ground in Death Valley.*

2201.10.04

Outside the compound in Cabo San Lucas, Premier Supreme Theo Zedera, General Lucan Desmond, and General Stephan Gruber relaxed on a vast, sun-splashed patio tiled in a yellow and red mosaic of costly Mexican ceramics. Scant yards away, surf added booming counterpoint to the Mozart piano concerto wafting over the deck. Intermittent tinkling laughter floated down from the open window of an upstairs room where Esten Balin was entertaining and being entertained by some of the women currently attending him.

All three men sitting in the luxurious Velex chairs on the patio wore sandals and swim trunks and tropical shirts. Desmond had already appeased the appetites Balin was satisfying upstairs, and now, eyelids lowered, he luxuriated in the warm breeze and gentle rays of the sun bathing his face, the fragrance of ocean and frangipani filling his nostrils, the day more intoxicating than the drinks on the extended arm of his chair. The Premier too sat quietly, lulled by the perfection of this day, the fingers of one hand occasionally moving to the music as he gave desultory attention to reports on his communicator.

Then, like a dog hearing a sound on some inaudible

frequency, he cocked his head and looked over to the doorway. Kenan Vartan emerged onto the patio in full uniform and saluted smartly. The Premier, his ebony eyes fastened intensely on Vartan, gave a curt nod, as did Desmond, who thought how ridiculous the salute would look were Vartan too wearing shorts and sandals.

"Sir," Vartan said, standing ramrod-straight, "you requested I report in person with any interim findings from the commander regarding sector sixty-nine—"

"Yes. Report," the Premier said, waving off further context. "And do stand at ease, General."

Vartan slightly spread his legs. "High velocity winds with indeterminate climate prediction factors due to volcanic activity, four point six percent visibility, abnormal reptilian life. Subterranean probing shows radioactivity indicators at forty-five, toxicity ratings at ninety-seven." Consulting his communicator, Vartan read, "Preliminary finding is no evidence of human life or possibility that human life could exist above or below ground in sector sixty-nine. Danger level of plus ten to men and equipment."

"Degree of reconnaissance?"

Vartan gave a scarcely discernible shrug. "At this point, sir, only twenty-three percent."

The Premier nodded, rubbing a hand across his chin. He turned his gaze to the sea, and his chagrin was visible to Desmond, who was surprised by it. The Premier rarely displayed reaction to military reports, receiving them with impassivity or, more frequently these days, sarcasm.

"I had a feeling, a suspicion," the Premier murmured. "Something like this would be..." He looked back at Vartan. "Have them complete their maneuvers in the most thorough manner possible under the conditions. I want—"

Another general, Levor Copeland, marched out onto the deck, saluted. "We have just received a surveillance anomaly in sector sixty-nine." His voice was pitched high with excitement.

2201.10.04—AFRICA

Joss.

What am I to do about Joss?

My first thought as I awaken, as I become aware of the astonishing fact that I have slept more deeply than I have in two years. As I become aware of the reasons why I feel refreshed and my body feels replete. As I realize that I am clothed again, that Joss has accomplished this while I slept. These thoughts even before the imperative of considering our present circumstances.

Unless a change in my breathing has alerted her, she does not appear to know I am awake. It is just dawn or perhaps slightly past—I can dimly make out her form in the deep grayness—and she is laying out provisions from our desert pak. I know I must assess the situation with our invaders but the greater urgency is what to do about her right now.

Supposedly I am the one with the sophistication. I am the one to take the lead and set the tone for the aftermath of our confounding night together.

There seems no limit to my capacity for transgression. I caused the events of this night and this quandary; my loss of control opened the way, my succumbing to the combination of Joss's welcoming gentleness and strength, my yearning for respite, for comfort, an easing of the burden that so unrelentingly crushes my soul. That I have yearned all my life, not just these past months, for the sweet loving moments I have now had in the arms of this tender, protective young woman excuses nothing.

I fear that damage to her has now been added to the list of my felonies. Especially considering Tara's feeling toward her—a devotion transparent to everyone except Joss. Assuming we survive these circumstances, I may now have set up an expectation from Joss toward me where there can be none.

Assuming we survive these circumstances. That is the only priority at this moment—it must be my focus. I will not address anything with her now. When Joss and I are safe, I will talk with her about what has transpired, and explain why any continuation of what has happened between us...however transportingly beautiful it was, and it was so very, very beautiful...is impossible, hopeless...

This much decided at least, I sit up. And say, simply, "Joss."

"Africa," she replies, and in her tone is a mere acknowledgment of my greeting. As if I had just entered a room. As if our encounter had been meaningless. Or perhaps already consigned to her personal history book. A reaction I should welcome but don't, and which altogether puzzles me. This young woman is a fount of surprises.

"They're breaking camp, nothing more," Joss informs me succinctly. "You need water. And something to eat."

Anyone would imagine eating or drinking to be impossible in view of this danger. But then, anyone would expect lovemaking to be equally improbable. Despite—perhaps because of—every effort at self-containment, control can fracture, and there will be no gainsaying the cravings of the body that overwhelm like the tides.

So, thirsty and ravenous, I force myself to slowly sip water as I nibble an energy tab and then a fruit packet, allowing time for this sustenance to flood my body with nourishment, to transmit to my brain the message of assuaged hunger.

Only then do I rise—on legs that contain tremulous echoes of their tension when they were clasped around Joss—to view the exterior world.

In the shadowy predawn, soldiers are barely visible performing morning rituals in an orderly process of breaking camp. In my immediate view is sand traveling in small, harmless-looking rivulets, a sight which pleases me greatly. This rising dawn wind indicates that as planned, Bannon Crater's mighty power and potential have been harnessed by my sisters.

Beside me, Joss freezes. I look over to her sector: Six soldiers approach. I too am paralyzed, my pulse escalating with each one of their purposeful strides toward us.

Taking my arm as she points, Joss whispers, "No weapons."

They do actually carry weapons, side arms, but she means they have no weapons drawn, that universal indication of overt suspicion or hostile intent.

"Unless you count those," she whispers again as the six unfasten and reach into their pants and then proceed to lavishly urinate all over our rock.

Through her hold on my arm I feel Joss shake with silent laughter. Imagining our sisters' hilarity at this display, I too would laugh were I not looking at the bulked-up, testosterone-enhanced body of the soldier who has removed his helmet and, disconcertingly, appears to be looking directly at me, his pale blue eyes glittering in vacant malignity from drug intoxication. Also, I see the gloved hands of several of the soldiers touching our abode, apparently for balance as they lean forward into the wind to urinate. If those in command are suspicious of the rock, this is a good ruse to gather chemical samples on the gloves to further analyze its composition without drawing notice.

This is allied to something of nagging concern to me. If, before and during this invasion, satellite range was converged and focused in ultra-high-definition scans with increased pass-over intervals on this area as part of the search, then they will have considerable imaging data for reference background. I tell myself that the entire Earth has already been mapped and remapped via high-definition scans throughout the duration of the search, and they would not perform such scans in advance of a direct, on-site search...but if they in fact have just rescanned with high definition, then this location will show up with the abode we occupy pinpointed as an anomaly. They will know that something is here that is not supposed to be here.

The soldiers finish and go on their way, leaving the hot pungent smell of themselves behind. But only momentarily, because of the erasing wind. As the gray of predawn lightens, Joss and I are braced and waiting for what we know will be next—the holograms we have worked so hard to create for this day. But as blowing sand thickens with the howling of the winds, we will have to trust to the skills and abilities of our sisters, because the sandstorm is rapidly rendering us blind...

2201.10.04—OLYMPIA

The situation feels odd, very odd to me.

The winds are slowly diminishing as the hot daytime land surface temperature takes hold to even out the temperature variant we have created. Accordingly, Tara has called for new coordinates to adjust some of our reptilian imagery. In keeping with the habits of each species we have caused some snakes to vanish, while some partially appear under rocks, while still others of the lizard family skitter over the landscape. It does not surprise me that the invaders in Rule Canyon, where the storm still rages in impressive fashion, remain immobilized. But all the activity in the encampment beside Faderman's View, where the weather has cleared sufficiently for troop movement, has also ceased. Unaccountably, by my lights.

But not by Tara's. She appears unconcerned. "Esteemed Olympia, undoubtedly they have sent in a preliminary report and await orders."

"They would have received detailed orders before their invasion. They await new orders?"

"Correct."

"Orders such as what?"

"To pull out, it is to be hoped," she says with just a trace of exasperation. Which I suppose I deserve. But she adds grimly, "The other possibilities are to change the parameters of their search, perhaps its depth." So, clearly, she is not entirely unconcerned.

If they expand rather than limit their search, then we are faced with a bleak prognosis: They will force the destruction of much, if not all of the home we have created with so much love and effort, such dedication.

The howling storm in Rule Canyon is now a mixed blessing. It has grounded our adversaries, true, but has also blurred to an indistinguishable mass all landscape features, including any images of the refuge that holds Africa and Joss. Our monitoring devices, acute as they are, cannot fully penetrate the fierce particle fusion that is now this sandstorm.

Although I place no less faith and trust in Tara's judgment than I do in Africa's, I do wish Africa were here so that I could be reassured by her overview and quiet wisdom, useful adjuncts that serve to reinforce Tara...

My intellect tells me that Africa and Joss must be safe. How could they not be? And that all is well in Rule Canyon. How could it not be?

Tara must, must be correct about the reasons why our invaders are hunkered down and waiting.

2201.10.04

On the patio of the Premier's compound in Cabo San Lucas, Desmond sat up straight in his chair at the excitement on General Levor Copeland's face.

"We feel the anomaly in sector sixty-nine is of significance," Copeland said.

"Report," the Premier said sharply.

"As you instructed four days ago, we converged satellite range and focused ultra-high-definition scans on the largest uninhabited areas only and increased pass-over intervals to every twenty-four hours. So we have considerable imaging data for reference background—"

"What *is* it, General?" the Premier barked.

"A surface anomaly. Sir, your communicator and General Desmond's have the two compared high-definition images, on priority transmission."

As Vartan and Gruber gathered around, Desmond set his communicator and projected the first three-dimensional image onto the patio floor.

The Mexican tiles mutated into a rocky, hamada-type desert, desolate, hilly, with exposed rock and strewn boulders and gravel, green splashes of creosote bush amid all the tans and grays—common desert terrain. Nearby this general area of Calivada, Desmond remembered from his briefings, close to two hundred nuclear tests had been detonated beneath the surface in the mid to late twentieth century, and the land had also been used as a bombing range. Then came the earthquakes leading to the poisoning of the western aquifer by nuclear contamination. Earthquakes could not have been unexpected this far inland—they had always been prevalent anywhere along the Pacific Rim. He was only somewhat knowledgeable in the field of bionomics, but even to a layman the shortsighted misuse of this land in previous times was breathtaking. The entire area, thousands of square miles, had become in effect an extended and permanent Death Valley.

Desmond laid out the next image, taken twenty-four hours later. Except for the military encampment at the edge of the image it looked identical, and Desmond would not have immediately noticed any other abnormality except for the violet color identifier.

"A rock," he said.

"Present in image two but not in image one," Gruber said, pointing as he crouched for a closer look.

The Premier was ahead of them both, already reading the data. "Dimensions at the furthest points are one point nine eight by two point one meters. General Copeland, do we have onsite readings?"

"We do, sir," said Copeland. "From the encampment's scanners, and an onsite sample taken by six soldiers who approached the anomaly on the pretext of urinating."

"Ingenious," Gruber said with a grin.

Copeland said, "Geological report is on track two."

"Igneous volcanic rock," Desmond read aloud from track two on his communicator. "Unusually high intergranular porosity. Fractures—intersecting planar discontinuities. Surface of widely distributed asperity heights. Electromagnetic impulse readings indicate high surface permeability. Not atypical for the terrain..." He abandoned any attempt to read the lists of minerals, composition, crystal system, and density.

"The core readings," the Premier said to Copeland. "I see none here."

Desmond never ceased to be impressed by the breadth of the Premier's knowledge and how far beyond his it went; even the summary information had been foreign to him.

Copeland replied, "These are the readings throughout, sir."

"Depth?"

A faint smile softened Copeland's features. "Nine centimeters."

The Premier was studying Copeland with his own beginnings of a smile. "Interesting."

"Our geologists say the same thing, sir."

"Who is in charge in sector sixty-nine, General?"

"Lieutenant General Jarvis."

"Excellent. Current status?"

"Sixty knot winds and ten meters visibility. The surface anomaly is under full surveillance with visual transmissions."

"Your orders to the Lieutenant General?"

"Force fields up, perimeter weapons at the ready, but do not fire, stand by at all cost, take no action whatsoever. Action on my command only."

The Premier nodded. "Excellent work, General Copeland. Extend my compliments to Lieutenant General Jarvis."

"Yes, sir. Thank you, sir." Copeland seemed to expand and glow under the Premier's approval, a phenomenon Desmond had witnessed often. Men would, and did, kill with alacrity for this man's approval, and Desmond was the first to admit he was one of them.

"And General," the Premier said, "I want the visual

transmissions sent directly to me immediately. You are dismissed."

Copeland smartly saluted, turned on his heel, and marched off.

The Premier turned to Desmond. "Lucan?"

Desmond shrugged. "A weapon of sabotage—that seems the strongest likelihood. It's an interesting weapon. We have no idea when the anomaly appeared within the satellite cycle, and it's less than a third of a kilometer from the campsite. It's what Copeland thinks too, why he's ordered force fields up."

"Stephan," the Premier said.

Gruber, Desmond had observed, had been shaking his head, scarcely able to contain his desire to interrupt and disagree with his commanding officer.

"If that were so, our incursion would need to have been anticipated," Gruber argued, his voice rising as he pointed to the images on the patio floor. "And preparations made on terrain deadly to human life—"

"Then what's its purpose?" Desmond disputed him mildly. "It's virtually within our encampment. Strongly suggesting surveillance, if not sabotage."

"Any ideas as to origin, Lucan? Have we seen anything like it before?"

"We have not," Desmond conceded.

The Premier was looking at Gruber reflectively. "You said our incursion would need to be anticipated. Maybe it wasn't, General. Maybe it was a surprise...a complete surprise."

Kenan Vartan spoke up for the first time. "A hideout," he said.

"Using features of the terrain as disguise," Gruber said.

"In that case," Vartan said, "any of the rocks in the area could be—"

"—hideouts as well," Gruber said. "All the rock needs

to be cleared out. Smashed down to the size of—"

"We can't," Vartan said emphatically. "We can't lay down laser fire in there."

"I wasn't suggesting we do," Gruber said in irritation. "We would need to—"

"Need to do what?" Esten Balin said, strolling out onto the patio, cigar in hand, his hairy body naked, an arm supporting an equally naked and staggeringly intoxicated blond.

"Esten," Stephan Gruber said, "we may soon be making full use of your second-best talent."

Grinning, Balin held his cigar to the stomach of the blond, who leaped away shrieking, her eyes wide in unbelieving shock and pain. Still screaming, she fled from the patio. Sickened, Desmond looked away. Always before this monster had confined his horrific deeds to his private laboratory.

"Esten, leave us," the Premier said coldly. "And put some clothes on."

Balin threw him a drunken salute and staggered off.

The Premier said to his generals, "Gentlemen, let's look at the composition data and climate conditions and plan our next step."

2201.10.04—JOSS

I knew Africa was awake long before she chose to reveal the fact to me. Which told me she was in turmoil over what had happened between us. I also realized that her focus must be on the peril confronting us, which is why it was essential that I lay out food to strengthen her for the uncertain hours that lie ahead, and why I behaved in so perfunctory a manner when she conceded she was awake.

Whatever happens now, I am fulfilled far beyond anything I could have dreamed. Most gratifying is that I was absolutely right about her, right about what I knew from the first moment I looked into her face when I was a child. All of her isolation, all of her loneliness—I felt it in her every embrace of me, her every moan this night. And I have given what I dreamed of giving all my life—I gave her comfort, and beyond that, pleasure.

In our hideaway we are now virtually blind, and have been so for perhaps two hours. But it is difficult to gauge time; we are in a state of near sensory deprivation. The wind's screams and roars have rendered conversation nearly impossible, and the sandstorm has darkened the day to predawn murkiness.

When I last could look into Africa's face I saw that if she was initially puzzled by my offhand behavior, she had sealed it from her thoughts and was again remote from me. She has shouldered her burdens and once more bears the weight of our Earth upon her. But for a timeless while I did hold that burden away from her, and I will always have within me the knowledge and the memory that for hours I held in my arms the most transcendent woman I will ever know.

She pulls on my arm and I lean close, my ear close to her lips to hear her shout, "Can you hear that?"

I strain to hear something, anything beyond the screaming of the wind, a wind that seems to threaten to dislodge our firmly rooted abode. Is that a roar beyond the roar? I cannot quite decide.

I do feel an actual tugging on our rock. I do hear roaring—the whine of a robotic arm. And then I hear Africa scream, scream so loudly that I hear her plainly despite the storm:

"We need to get out! Now!"

2201.10.04—OLYMPIA

The storm has lifted slightly over Rule Canyon, enough to give us somewhat improved visibility. But a much worse storm has descended on our Unity.

The rock-like shell containing Africa and Joss has vanished.

The most thunderstruck of any of us is Tara. Pale and shaken, she simply gapes at the blowing sand burying all traces of the hideout's previous location.

Her demeanor impinges not at all on our confidence in her ability as our leader, which has been proven in full measure during these past two years; still, we are all of us in shock at this latest development. The event, however, has evidently impinged on my own intelligence because I have already stupidly asked her, "What happened?"

And she has given the only conceivable answer, delivering it tersely: "I don't know."

Our consternation is beyond my power to describe. Except for our children, who play in undisturbed innocence in their chamber, our entire Unity stands virtually immobile, many of them close around us, others anxiously in front of the screens throughout this vast amphitheater. We must discuss this dire new emergency and make a decision. Isis and I, along with Vellmar, Rakel, Rozene, Viridia, and Raina, gather around our leader.

"Let's examine the situation, the possibilities, our course of action," Tara addresses us, her support team, and our Unity. Her voice is firm. "There appear to be three feasible reasons for what's happened. One is that our invaders acted under the cover of this storm—a storm that would have rendered the invaders equally invisible to Joss and Africa as it did to us." Her voice trembles as she adds, "And during that time they perhaps had cause to destroy some of the landscape, and the abode with Africa and Joss along with it."

As we contemplate this unpalatable scenario, Vellmar says, "This is most certainly not the case." Her authority for making so unequivocal a statement is unassailable: She is the hideout's creator. "The shell is designed to withstand all weaponry save laser fire," she reminds us, "and had they used such weapons, they would have left blast marks on the surrounding terrain, and a catastrophic chain reaction would have already begun. Our readings show toxicity levels unchanged."

Tara nods but does not look relieved. "The second possibility is that our invaders somehow identified the hideout as an anomaly. If so, no storm would have stopped them from removing it."

"They'd chart its coordinates," Rakel says slowly, as she puts the ramifications of this statement of Tara's together. "Then seize it whole. Extract it from the desert with retractors from a hovercraft high above the storm..."

She does not finish and does not need to. This scenario would mean Africa and Joss have been captured. An eventuality unthinkable in its implications.

"Then there's the third alternative," Tara says, and at the hope in her tone I feel my own hope rise even before she speaks. "Africa and Joss acted on their own, dissolved and abandoned their hideout under the cover of the storm for reasons unknown to us, and have concealed themselves elsewhere."

"They couldn't tell us," Isis continues eagerly. "They couldn't communicate with us."

"Not even if they wanted to," Vellmar agrees. "Not when we shut down their communicators after our Mayday call."

"We dare not activate them under any circumstance," Rakel says. "If Africa and Joss are safely hidden, we dare not run the risk of exposing them by activating their communicators."

"But," Tara says somberly, "if the second possibility is correct, and they've captured Africa and Joss, then we face the gravest possible danger. No matter how determined they may be not to divulge information, no matter how willing they may be to suffer and die rather than reveal what they know, the information about our whereabouts will be gained from them..." The agony in Tara's voice is such that I can only marvel at her ability to lay out these facts. "They will soon know where we are if they do not know already."

And we are all of us as good as dead. A thought that does not need to be voiced.

"But if they have not been captured," Raina ventures, "then Africa and Joss are on their own out there in our valley. Somewhere."

"So the question comes down to this," Isis says. "What do we do now?"

"And the answer," Tara replies, "is obvious to us all."

Clearly it is. Because I hear a resounding chorus of voices in a unanimous vote: "We wait."

And hope.

2201.10.04

In the compound at Cabo San Lucas, Desmond strode hurriedly down the corridor toward the Premier's quarters. Humming a jaunty tune, he flung an equally jaunty salute at the sentries beside the Premier's doorway. They returned his salute like the barely human robots they were, gazes fixed on the rayscans over their eyes that X-rayed and tox-screened every person who ventured down this hallway, their earscopes modulated to the readings and any command issued from the exterior perimeter protecting the Premier, or from the Premier himself.

Under any circumstances they would have no way of knowing what a great day this was. Outside of a very small, closed circle no one in the world knew, not even the Premier. Desmond had made sure of that, had called upon all of his command powers, had made enough subtle threats that he was confident Esten Balin and Stephan Gruber were being fed a loop of delayed information. Only Desmond had the true facts, all of the current data relating to the rock shelter having been funneled through him, and the news was so momentous that he had to deliver it in person. Only he and those on the recovering ship, under the command of General Levor Copeland, knew the full story, and they were shielded in a force field and a state of complete lockdown while awaiting his orders.

This was perhaps the greatest day since the Takeover. No, there was no "perhaps" about it. This date was unquestionably the one from which he would measure his first totally unfettered enjoyment of the fruits of his loyalty and service to Theo Zedera.

Desmond passed under the DNA scanner and for the first time did not tense in awareness of its instantaneous judgment and destructive power. He entered the clicked-open door into the Premier's quarters, marching briskly across the royal-blue carpet.

Esten Balin was not at his post. Unusual. But fortunate. He himself would have the pleasure of imparting this stunning piece of news to the Premier, unadulterated by Balin's brutish presence. He saluted, and stood at attention in eager anticipation.

The Premier, a vista of surf cascading outside his windows, was pacing behind his desk, communicator in hand, his face clouded with thought. "At ease, Lucan," he greeted Desmond distractedly, and placed his communicator on the desk as if he had just noticed he held it. "It's good of you to come. So we have caught ourselves the biggest and best possible fish."

Desmond was staggered. And speechless. Zed *knew.* How could he already know?

The Premier was studying him. "I'm astonished and extremely pleased by the news, as I'm sure you imagine."

"Who—"

"General Gruber notified me about three minutes ago."

Gruber. *Gruber.* And Copeland...Gruber could not have done this without Copeland. Desmond dropped his gaze but was unable to conceal his fury; he knew his face was betraying him.

"All will be well, Lucan," the Premier said gently.

Desmond looked sharply at him. There was a softening—pity perhaps?—in the Premier's face, and this was a tone he had never before heard from Zed. The Premier continued, "I've asked him to present himself."

The door clicked open as someone passed through the DNA scanner, and Gruber entered the room. Slim and elegant in his formal dress whites, he marched to the Premier's desk, halted, smartly saluted.

"At ease," the Premier said. He was leaning over his desk, focused on a touch pad.

Looking pleased with himself, Gruber spread his feet. He did not look at Desmond. But Desmond was far more interested in the two black-clad, armed sentries who had lithely, silently followed Gruber, passing through the DNA scanner without being annihilated. They took up positions flanking the door inside the room, their opaque helmet visors down. Never, never had he seen anyone bearing weapons of any kind in the Premier's presence. It was not permitted, had never been permitted, and for anyone stupid or careless enough to bring weapons through an established perimeter the penalty was death without appeal, carried out immediately.

"A moment," the Premier said. He carefully tapped three times on the touch pad, then seated himself in his high-backed chair, leaned back, and placed a foot up on the corner of his desk. The Premier, Desmond noted with increasing unease, had invited neither Gruber nor himself to sit.

"General Gruber," the Premier said, steepling his fingers, "your news was most welcome."

Desmond was surprised by the formal use of Gruber's title; the Premier had been calling him by first name for many weeks. Gruber also looked startled. "I knew you'd be—" He caught himself. "Indeed, sir."

"And Mr. Balin? Does he also know?"

"Yes, sir, I've advised him. I assumed you would want him to immediately prepare his instruments for the questioning process."

The Premier nodded. "Yes, of course that would be something you'd assume. General Gruber, one interesting aspect of your news is that it came from you. Instead of Supreme General Desmond."

Gruber smiled easily and favored Desmond with a glance. "An accident, I'm sure. I've developed my own sources of information. As a failsafe system, of course."

Desmond's anger had gone, replaced by apprehension. Tensely, warily, he angled himself so that he could observe the motionless sentries as he listened to this interchange between the Premier and Gruber.

"It's my opinion," the Premier said, "based on observation of you over the past months, that in developing your own channels of information you've succeeded in undermining your commanding officer."

"That was not my intent, sir." The smile faded from Gruber's aristocratic features. "It was I who developed the profile of Ferdinand the Messiah. I who provided other information I believe you've found quite useful. After all, Supreme General Desmond has the same access—"

The Premier raised a hand. "Yes. Indeed. And I value the information, and I value intelligence, initiative, and ambition."

Gruber smiled again.

He's going to kill me, Desmond realized. Zed's brought those sentries in to kill me right here. To give Gruber the satisfaction of watching it happen.

"I value loyalty even more, General Gruber. And I do not value an overweening ambition whose work product is disloyalty. Nor do I value your assumption of authority in suggesting to Mr. Balin what you think I might wish him to do."

"But, sir—"

Seeing the Premier's dark gaze shift to a point behind him, Gruber broke off and looked around, seeing the sentries for the first time. His jaw slackened.

"It's merely one more step, General Gruber, from assuming what I would instruct Mr. Balin to do to actually having him do it. And one additional step to assuming that everything I decide can be just as easily and perhaps better decided by you."

"Sir, that's just not true!" Gruber's voice rose in shrill insistence. "I've never—"

The Premier nodded to the sentries. "Proceed," he said.

Gruber instinctively clawed at the side of his uniform, seeking the firearm that was not there. "I—" He broke off, apparently realizing that words were now futile. As the sentries simultaneously raised their weapons, he audibly sucked in his breath.

They fired precise, short bursts that blazed holes, briefly red, then black, into the chest area of Gruber's white uniform. As he staggered, their fire followed his body to the carpet, continuing until his writhing ceased.

"Remove him," the Premier said.

The sentries, standing on either side of Gruber's body, lifted him up by the arms and dragged him across the carpet to the doorway. A sudden brilliance stung Desmond's eyes as the three figures were outlined in the doorway and bathed in laser fire. In less than a second the brilliance vanished; dust swirled in a wild dance that would end only when the exhausted particles floated onto the floor.

Desmond understood that when the Premier had made those three taps he had reprogrammed the DNA scanner to reject and destroy all three men as soon as the sentries with Gruber's body exited the room. Three taps—Gruber and the two sentries. Not four. Desmond slowly exhaled. Unless the Premier changed his mind, Desmond would leave this room alive.

The Premier, who had not removed his foot from the corner of his desk during the entire event, gestured toward the swirling dust and said musingly, "I learned from Premier Zhou in China that people whom you distrust, but who nevertheless have indispensable value to you, you keep them as close as you safely can. To watch them. The instant they are of no further value, you discard them."

"I see, sir," Desmond said.

"I value your service, Lucan."

"Yes, sir. I see that too. Thank you, sir." He would do anything for this man. Anything. Not because he feared him, which he fulsomely did, but because he loved the pitiless clarity of mind that illuminated every problem and then reduced it to its harshest elements.

"You may do as you wish with General Copeland," the Premier said. "As long as the result is death."

"Yes, sir," Desmond said. Balin, he would give Copeland to the tender mercies of Esten Balin. No. He would simply sign an execution order for Copeland and his entire circle of personal advisers. He would never give anyone to Esten Balin.

The Premier swung his foot down from the desk and turned his chair toward the window, opening it to the sounds of ocean beyond it, sitting in profile to Desmond. Desmond waited. Zed had not formally dismissed him. For obvious reasons.

"The prisoners," the Premier said.

"They remain sedated, sir. Medical scans—"

"Yes. Beyond that." The Premier's gaze remained fixed on the roiling, thudding surf.

Desmond understood that Zed wanted not the end result of the extraction operation but the full story. "We got to them not a moment too soon. Even under cover of a screaming sandstorm they'd figured out what was going on and managed to get out—"

"Yes." The Premier's full lips twitched briefly. "She would have known, have realized... Go on, Lucan."

"We found them outside their shell, which had only partly collapsed behind them, indicating their haste. We—"

"So they were desperate."

"Very desperate. We had them encapsulated, our narcotic-infused hermetic seal around the shell, but the younger one managed to wedge her desert pak into one of the seals—"

The Premier jerked his head around to Desmond. "That's impossible."

"Yes, supposedly. It shows you their determination to escape. And they might have succeeded were they not overcome by the narcotics before enough outside air could get in."

"Had they succeeded..."

Desmond shrugged. "In all likelihood they'd have died in the storm. Or managed to dig themselves in and made things more complicated for us. For a time. Until conditions allowed us to bring full instrumentation to bear on pinpointing them. There was no possibility of eluding us, of course."

"They would have killed themselves by then," the Premier observed.

Desmond shrugged again. "I suppose they would have, sir. To avoid questioning." He pushed away the thought of the fate that now awaited them in Balin's hands.

"What are your current orders to General Copeland?"

"To keep them sedated. They have been fully processed and separated by force field, of course, to prevent one from using the other for suicide. The extraction team is awaiting further orders."

"Physical condition?"

"Our scans indicate excellent." Meaning that Balin could extend their torture for a very long time. He reluctantly asked, "Your orders, sir?"

"General Copeland is to deliver them here with the hermetic seal intact. You may then dispose of him as you choose."

"The execution order for him and his staff will be carried out immediately afterward, sir."

The Premier nodded. "The expeditionary force in sector sixty-nine. Under no circumstances are they to take action of any kind until they receive orders coded with my seal. As for the prisoners, I want them placed in this room. Immediately. And revived here. I want you on hand during and after the installation and revival process."

"Sir, may I point out the dangers of having them right here in your—"

"You may not. Now, as for Balin," the Premier said.

"Yes, sir," he said, hoping Zed would not force him to watch Balin with these women.

"He is to be executed immediately."

"Yes sir," Desmond managed to say.

"He's out of control."

He's always been out of control, Desmond thought. There was another reason, there had to be. Perhaps Zed knew of or suspected a cabal with Gruber and Copeland.

"I could perhaps simply have him come to this office, Lucan," the Premier said thoughtfully, gesturing to the doorway.

Desmond said quietly, "I'll be glad to personally carry out your wishes regarding Mr. Balin, sir."

The Premier smiled. "I thought perhaps you might be."

2201.10.04—OLYMPIA

As if our situation—our peril—is not extreme enough...now this. Now this astounding development.

A signal has just come over the Interplanetary Frequency Channel. Into the emergency receptor-beacon rooted deep under the land we occupy. Its four-pulse rhythm reverberates on the terminal, the message eloquent, unmistakable. And our Unity is in utter disarray.

When we came here, the previously agreed-upon priority was to entomb immediately an IFC device, an exact match for those in governmental and space research agencies in numerous other areas around the globe. But the labor of concealing it was carried out in the assumption that the odds of its implementation in specific regard to us were vanishingly small.

Impossible, of course, to know the source—inside or outside the solar system—of this contact. The coordinates of signal activation were designed and encased in scattershot micro-engineered encryption by the finest minds among us to frustrate trace by our enemies; and the design also created the necessary side effect of shutting out any hope of direct trace by ourselves.

Impossible to doubt the authenticity of the signal: It has cut off after nine repetitions. The number chosen for its symbolism: to represent the number of Mother's original offspring...

The hubbub among our Unity has finally quieted. An expression of the utmost gravity on her face, Tara rises to address us.

"It is, of course, from our sisters," she confirms. "We cannot know whether it is from some or all of them. We have no means of knowing where they are, but in all likelihood they transmit from safety somewhere beyond the Einsteinian Curve."

I hope and trust this is true, that she is not being optimistic.

"We must make a decision immediately," Tara says grimly. "We have not a moment to lose. We have two choices. To respond...or not."

Hands on her hips, she paces before us as she lays out the facts. "If we respond, our signal will eventually be traced to us and will confirm we're here. At the very least, it will provide more evidence for our enemies to locate us. However, if they've captured Africa and Joss, or have found their bodies, our invaders may know this already."

Unspoken, not needing to be spoken, is the naked fact that our invaders have not left our valley. They are hunkered down and appear to be awaiting orders.

When no one offers rebuttal, Tara continues. "If we do not respond, that will in itself achieve the result of sending a message to our sisters. Of distress."

Isis says from beside me, "That may result in bringing our sisters here, to investigate our lack of response."

"Would they do that?" Rakel asks. "They face the same military might that pursued them when they left."

"That would not deter them. They would not use the *Amelia Earhart* or a ship like it," Tara points out. "Undoubtedly they would take small shuttle craft to elude discovery, just as they used Kendra's service ships to travel to the main ship for their escape—"

Rakel interrupts. "They would of course see the damage to Earth from the air—"

"—but have no concept of the changes since they left, the search for us, what lies in wait for them." Tara crosses her arms and simply waits.

In the silence that follows this statement, I am profoundly aware, to the depths of my soul, that Isis and I are the representatives of Mother on this planet, the elders of her progeny. I look at my beloved sister, into the sweetly aged face with its fine lines of experience and wisdom, and see in her eyes the same awareness of this, and also the fateful message I knew would be there, the message I needed to see to lend me the courage to speak.

I, Olympia the historian, rise and say in my firmest tones to Tara, to our entire Sisterhood here on Earth: "We must signal them Condition Nine."

Our highest level of emergency. Nine consecutive pulses, repeated nine times.

Do not proceed under any circumstance.

Transmitting the Condition Nine code will also mean our death sentence—the ending of even our faintest of hopes of survival.

Tara takes my hand. "We cannot save ourselves," she says. "Let us save our sisters."

All of our Sisterhood joins hands.

Our vote is unanimous.

2201.10.04—JOSS

It has been two hours since I awoke. In a detention cube, with my body floating on a cushion of compressed air. Even without opening my eyes I knew my heavy-headedness was narcotic-induced and would quickly end—I could smell the distinctive astringency of airborne stim. Clearly, it was useless to resist wakefulness or to feign sleep: My body functions were being monitored by the sensor I could feel implanted on the crown of my head, and my "mattress" was swiftly dissipating beneath me.

I knew the stim was being pumped in through a complex set of sieve-like vents far too extensive in area for me to block had I wanted to. I had discovered this when we were narcotized however many hours—perhaps even days—ago. I was helpless to resist any chemical controllant. Aside from having been drugged, I seemed to be intact, unharmed.

Lying on the plasticine floor of the cube, I opened my eyes, took in my immediate vicinity. The cube was entirely transparent, and barren of anything except myself. My desert pak was gone, as were my wrist pak and boots, and my clothes had been affixed to my body to defeat any determination of mine to remove them for any purpose.

After taking the time to cautiously look further around

me and confirm that our circumstances were indeed every millimeter as dire as I'd expected, in fact even worse than I could have dreamed, I sat up and turned my attention to Africa. Suspended on her own air mattress, she lay on her side facing me, her body subtly stirring into wakefulness but her eyes still shut. She might as well have been in another country for all my access to her; I could see rippling edges of the force field separating us. Her air suspension was already dissolving and she was receiving her own dose of stim, but as she floated down to the floor she struggled toward consciousness as if it were eluding her—or perhaps she was the one resisting consciousness. I could easily sympathize with either alternative.

She made a slight groaning sound of protest as her body settled onto the floor—which told me that the force field between us was not, thankfully, of the soundproofing type—then blinked open her eyes and stared into mine. I saw through the twin reflections of myself into ebony depths, saw into the vulnerability of her, saw recognition and awareness and then horror inhabit her.

"Joss," she whispered. "Oh, Joss."

I knew her concern was not for herself or even our circumstances—it was entirely for me. I whispered back, "Africa, I'll be all right."

It was the truth. All I could do for her I had already done, and we were now in the maw of the monster. All control of our fate had passed from our hands into his. If I had learned anything from my reading of history it was that the only remaining course for us now was to look for any opportunity to deflect, however slightly, the course of that fate.

Although I knew it was futile, I tried to hold her gaze as if to mesmerize her, tried to stretch out every second I possibly could to postpone her need to glance away from me, the glance that would take in for the first time our horrific circumstances. But stim was pouring into her side of our cubicle, increasing her alertness, and of course she did look away, and I followed her gaze.

Outside our transparent cube, which had been placed on a vast expanse of royal-blue carpet in a room filled with opulent furnishings and walls of artwork and statuary, the first object in her line of vision was the ramrod-straight figure positioned beside us as if on guard, although he had no visible weapons and his attention was focused away from us. Dark-haired, tall, handsome, and powerfully built, he bore the five-bar red insignia of a general emblazoned on the breast of his black and gold uniform.

Dismayed recognition of him registering in her eyes, she looked beyond the uniformed man to where his attention was drawn, to the wide windows and the huge marble desk and the man seated there, his gray-blue tunic blending into the ocean rolling behind him. The most feared man in the universe.

The expressions on her face were changing too rapidly for me to read. I myself was still unsettled from when I had first looked at him. He had been contemplating the unconscious form of his former colleague and lifelong friend, and he shifted his gaze to me, held me transfixed as if a force beam had enveloped me. His eyes, identical to Africa's in their almond shape and ebony color, contained the elementary and absolutely arctic evaluation of a shark. He held and released me within the space of a second, returning his gaze to Africa. My few moments of further observing him revealed other subtle similarities besides eye color between these two formerly inseparable friends: the same straight line of shoulder, the same physical stillness in the way they sat, the slightly tilted, listening angle of head—undoubtedly born of their mutual experience in diplomacy. Save for the difference in skin color, they might have been twins, one of those classical representations of good and evil from my readings of mythology.

The room was so quiet, closed off—regrettably—even to the sound of ocean, that I assumed it had been Fluxbar-treated. There were no other soldiers visible, no weapons pointed at our cubicle, which of course did not mean that we were not under a virtual arsenal of unseen firepower.

Theo Zedera leaned forward. And broke the silence. "Africa," he said, and I was shocked by the huskiness of his voice, its sweet tenderness of tone.

"Theo," she replied, and if I live a thousand years I will never be able to describe the amalgam of grief and reproach and contempt and anger and anguish in that one word.

He said softly, "No one has called me by that name in a good long while."

"I'm sure not." Africa's voice had strengthened, taken on a pitch of surety. "I'm sure they call you monster. Murderer."

"At the very least," he replied, and sat up straight and gestured to the uniformed man. "General Desmond, I'm sure you remember Africa Contrera."

"Of course, sir."

"Africa, perhaps you remember General Desmond from the days when he commanded the Peacekeeper Corps."

"General Desmond," she said, not deigning to divert her eyes from the man at the desk, "I assume you've concocted a convincing rationalization for your betrayal of the world's trust and faith in you."

He did not flinch from her acid disdain. "I am proud of my service to the Premier," he said evenly, "and regret none of it."

Theo Zedera said, "He is my second in command, Africa, with the title of Supreme General."

"Ah, yes. The Supreme General to the Premier Supreme. And we both know how titles puff up mediocrity."

He did not react to her derision. "Africa, I don't know your companion's name."

Her eyes seeming even darker with her fury, Africa said to me, "Did you ever imagine that a display of such finely honed manners could emerge from such abomination?"

"My name is Joss," I offered. The display of etiquette by this man under these circumstances was as chilling as it was preposterous, and there was no point in not telling him my name. There was nothing to be gained by Africa's invective, or her rage, however justifiable. Perhaps a faint possibility existed that in some way I could reach him in his psychosis, that somehow I could prevent him from doing something unspeakable to Africa...

"Theo, you will not hurt Joss," Africa said, and there was more steeliness and command in her voice than I had ever heard even from Tara.

"I have a purpose for her," Theo Zedera said.

"Meaning?"

"Patience has always been one of your virtues," he said. "All will be—"

"Sir." The interruption from General Desmond was a peremptory order. Holding a hand up for silence, he touched the vicinity of his ear, evidently an implanted receiver, and looked at his wrist communicator.

"A code one alert. The buffer zone at the Einsteinian Curve has been penetrated. An incipient incursion into our solar system."

"Details," snapped the Premier.

"Few as yet, sir," said Desmond, pressing on his ear as he watched his communicator. "They remain beyond identification range. But they have transmitted a message. An exact sequence of four pulses repeated nine times. It has no known significance."

I don't know who was more shocked, Africa or myself. Perhaps Africa, who literally gaped at me.

Fortunately, Theo Zedera's attention was focused on Desmond. "It has significance to someone. Scan reports?"

Desmond shook his head. "Alien technology. They elude our scanning by scattering, absorbing, scrambling, and retransmitting our scans back to us. Unless they penetrate the EC they remain outside our capacity for identification and intercept. Their signal may indicate they're benign—"

"Or that they're hostile. We have no idea about their intent, Lucan. Assessment, Africa?"

I should not have been shocked that he asked. After all, this was exactly the kind of work they used to do together. I expected more caustic contempt from her, and was surprised when she shrugged; then I realized that she was still stunned by the news and probably did not trust her voice.

General Desmond said, "Our demand for identification has been transmitted—no response. Unmanned intercepts have been launched from Mars Base. Satellite defense has been activated. All bases are on automatic alert for further orders."

The Premier nodded. He was now watching Africa, not his general.

"Sir," General Desmond said. "Another message. Transmitted over the IFC—Earth origin. Sender unknown."

"*Earth* origin?" The Premier looked astonished. "Encrypted?"

"No, sir. A pattern of nine pulses. Also repeated nine times."

Africa and I exchanged glances, and something like a grim smile passed over her features, the barest nod. *It is the correct response,* she was telling me. *The correct decision.* I could only agree. My mother, my sister could be part of this astounding contact from space. The Mother of us all could be part of it...

"Origin?"

"That's what's encrypted, sir. We're working on it."

"Meaning you'll be days finding out."

Desmond gave a reluctant nod. "But with all our triangulation techniques we'll indeed have it."

"An invasion from space, Theo," Africa said. "How inconvenient for you."

He shocked me with his laugh, rich and hearty. Like sunlight suddenly illuminating a dark winter landscape. Even General Desmond looked taken aback.

"Since they've used the IFC," the Premier said to Africa, "more likely they're a trade freighter or a research vessel, not the space barbarians of our childhood imagination."

"Theo," she said, "a response has been sent to them."

At first I thought she simply could not help making a reply. Then I saw her strategy: to see what his own assessment might be.

He answered, "Maybe it's an attempt from a resistance movement to the Takeover to make a connection with an off-world civilization. Perhaps this incursion is an investigation in response to an original signal they managed to transmit out of our solar system despite our deflection shield." He shrugged. "Even if this is so, an alien civilization so technologically advanced knows that interference is useless. Nothing is more futile than empire-building."

Africa leaped into this opening. "A lesson lost on one particular person on our own planet."

To this tart response, this direct hit, the Premier merely

shrugged again. "You, Africa, know better than anyone that reality is seldom exactly what it seems. Before we talk further, and at the risk of further affronts to my manners, what can I reasonably do to make you more comfortable?"

Africa crossed her arms, contemptuous silence her reply. As for me, I squelched the terrified child in me that wanted to scream *Let us out of this cage!* and listened to the adult who understood very well that I would probably not survive this day, and that a swift death was the best outcome I could wish for. So I decided to ask for something that would fit his definition of reasonable. I said, "Would you open your window?" I would face my death with something wonderful to remember—the sound, if not the smell, of the ocean.

The Premier turned to me and, surprisingly, the coldness was gone from his eyes; they still contained evaluation, yes, but something else as well. Which I could not identify. He touched his desk and the windows behind him vanished and I saw and heard the crash of a wave and could have wept with the joy of it.

"Sir, we have another signal..." General Desmond waited, listening. "From our visitors outside the EC."

Impatiently, Theo Zedera picked up his own communicator. "It's in code," he said, frowning.

"A very ancient code. Morse code. And just a single word. What do you make of it, Lucan?"

Desmond shook his head. "It's in no known lexicon. I have no idea, sir."

"Nor do I."

I could no longer stand it. "What is it?" I blurted. "What's the word?"

"*Phosh,*" answered the Premier. "The word is *phosh.*"

Africa and I looked at each other. Not much wonder

the word was not in any lexicon. Only one person in the universe used that word. And it had only one meaning.

Mother—the Mother of us all—could not have chosen a more inopportune time to return to Earth. And the one-word message she had sent in reply to our *Do not proceed under any circumstance* command meant that she was not taking no for an answer.

2201.10.04

Throughout this day Desmond had felt an uneasiness bordering on disorientation. During all his time at the side of the Premier, even though he might not have fully understood the rationale behind Zed's orders, he could see the broad outlines of Zed's general approach and purpose, and the mind at work. But now, with each order received—or not received—from the Premier, he experienced a further loosening of even this much context. From the moment the anomaly had been discovered in sector sixty-nine Desmond had lost his grasp of what was happening. The Premier's behavior made no sense militarily or logically; the nonresponse or outright dismissals of his queries were raising his anxiety and bewilderment to high new levels. He had men to command, important duties to perform. He needed to understand; it was critical he understand what was happening and why.

Here he stood in the Premier's office with a Code One security alert blinking on his communicator—a breach of Earth's solar system perimeter unprecedented for the mystery surrounding this potential intrusion—and the Premier's reaction was unconcern. If not indifference. His focus was totally on these two women prisoners in the cage in his office, a priority that made no sense whatsoever other than being one more manifestation of obsession—

obsession that now seemed to border on madness. Opening the windows at the request of the woman named Joss was more important than dealing lucidly with a Code One security breach?

What did Zed intend to do with these women? Since Balin had been taken out of the equation, apparently torture for extraction of information had been taken out as well; but why weren't they being questioned by chemical means—equally effective and infallible for specific questions? And in any case, wasn't it clear that the Disappearance had been solved, that the rest of the women were secreted underground in sector sixty-nine and its environs? Now that the Disappearance had been solved, Desmond urgently needed to issue the orders around preliminary action, get some pieces into place.

For that matter, what about Ferdinand the Messiah? The capture of one of his inner group had been an unqualified success, the man taken down with surgical precision in an isolated situation with no witnesses. Balin had taken over, and what was left of the unfortunate had been placed in his house; the entire neighborhood and several adjacent ones were incinerated, punished for "resistance"—collateral damage to cover Zed's tracks.

What was Ferdinand the Messiah's "end of the world" date and what did it presage? The date was known only by Balin and the Premier... Perhaps he could still get the information from Balin.

Desmond quickly checked his communicator. Balin was too near death. Only the Premier now knew the date. If the date was imminent, then he needed to act on that front as well. The need to act on all of these fronts was urgent.

Desmond decided to make another attempt at gaining the Premier's attention. "Sir, your orders regarding the Code One—"

The Premier fastened an irritated stare on him. "Unless this visitor exceeds all known laws of science, a journey from the Einsteinian Curve to Earth orbit requires eighteen days. The action taken by the commanders on the scene is appropriate and sufficient for the present."

"But, sir—"

"It is sufficient, General."

Zed's clear annoyance, his formal use of Desmond's title were warning enough, but Desmond felt compelled to push on. "Sir, now that we have isolated where the women have concealed themselves, I recommend that we reinforce the troops in sector sixty-nine, send in additional weapons, perhaps have in place toxic gas pumps or saturation narcotics that will—"

"Status quo, General," the Premier said sharply. "On pain of *death*, your men are not to move a muscle until I command it. Is that clear?"

"Completely, sir," Desmond said, shocked.

"Balin," the Premier said. "Have you carried out my order?"

"It's being taken care of, sir."

In this, at least, he could take satisfaction, and he savored his actions. First, sealing off Balin's quarters to eliminate all possibility of escape. Entering those quarters with three carefully selected aides, all of them having ingested reaction-enhancing drugs. Balin, standing at a sheet-draped table from which pressure belts hung, obviously waiting for delivery of the prisoner Africa Contrera, and looking up with obscene eagerness as the portal to his theater opened. But they had not taken him by surprise. Immediately sizing up the situation, he had lunged for one of his instruments. Desmond easily shot him with parathane and took him down, Balin falling like a tree but fighting the paralytic drug all the way to the floor. The three aides had seized and held him until the futile struggle ended.

"By personal order of Premier Supreme Theo Zedera," Desmond informed him, smiling, "I am designated to carry out your execution."

Balin could make only guttural sounds through his frozen throat, but they were baleful and emanated fury, as did the expression in his eyes.

"For an inhuman scum like you," Desmond added, "this isn't execution, this is extermination."

Desmond raised the standard-issue laser gun he had requisitioned for the execution but saw only defiance, only contempt in Balin's eyes. Hesitating, holding the gun, he looked at the table covered with the white sheet, the belts hanging down, the gleaming surgical knives and drills and prods neatly arranged for Africa Contrera.

He holstered the gun. "Put him there," he said to his aides.

They obeyed with alacrity, hoisting him up and binding him tightly to the table. The paralytic drug was already beginning to wear off, and Balin was again struggling, this time to find his voice.

"I delegate the execution order to you," he told the aides.

"Yes, *sir,*" one of them said with enthusiasm, eyeing the instruments.

"Desmond—" Balin uttered. And befouled Desmond with a stream of curses.

"Take your time," Desmond said to the aides.

Scant minutes later Desmond saw the panic beginning to inhabit Balin's eyes. When he left the room the aides had begun work on Balin's genitals, and Balin was bucking against his bonds and screaming. That had been two hours ago.

"Lucan," the Premier said, "you say it's being taken care of. Is he...is it concluded?"

Understanding that the Premier's questions were couched in a manner to spare the women's sensibilities, Desmond again consulted his communicator. "Almost," he said. "It is being carried out with his own...implements."

"Very appropriate."

The Premier nodded toward the cube. "Would you have someone retrieve and deliver the personal recorders that belong to Africa and Joss?"

"Yes, sir," Desmond said, and he felt another lurch of disorientation.

2201.10.04—JOSS

Theo Zedera has had formachairs moved into our cube for our comfort. He has personally selected a variety of food and drink for us from his own dispenser, none of which I've touched, nor has Africa. In this surreal setting, Africa has disdained the proffered chair and sits on the floor on her side of our cube with her arms around her knees, a figure of impeccable tidiness in her earth-toned trouser suit and halo of dark hair as she stares at the man who works at his desk tapping on a series of touch pads in deep concentration, with the ocean, the eternal ocean, rolling behind him.

Like Africa, General Desmond, seated just outside our cube, watches the Premier in between constantly checking his communicator. Although I know nothing about the general, to me this man looks unsettled, discomfited, if not baffled by what has thus far transpired in this room.

As for me, I have settled myself in my chair and profitably used the time after Theo Zedera ordered General Desmond to return our personal recorders.

Now I too wait. General Desmond is surely no more puzzled than I about what awaits us. But he sits on the other side of our prison, and he shares none of our fear.

"My apologies," the Premier finally says, looking up at us. "I had urgent work to finish."

"The slaughter of more millions?" Africa inquires.

Theo Zedera gets up from his chair, moves toward us in an easy stroll. I have seen him hundreds of times on vidscreens, always imposing, engaging, magnetically intelligent and articulate; but he is smaller in person, a husky male of merely average height, and looks like any other male in his gray-blue tunic and dark pants, if you overlook the incongruity of velvet slippers. It is his head that draws, that dominates, as it does in all the video transmissions, large and fully finished with handsome, florid features, dark eyes, long lashes, aquiline nose, full lips...

I know this man is a monster. He does not seem like one. Or at least my notion of one.

He sits down in a chair beside his general and contemplates us, chin in hand. "Africa," he finally says into a room filled with silence save for the crashing of surf, "you still haven't asked the obvious question."

"You know I don't ask obvious questions, Theo. Especially when they have obvious answers. And the obvious answer is, you're a psychopath."

"If that's so," he says softly, steepling his fingers, "how I could pass all the scanner tests and show no sign of brain abnormality?"

"I've wondered about that," she admits. "How *did* you manage it?"

He turns his gaze to me. "Joss, I note that Africa is not employing her recorder."

"I see no point in doing so," Africa retorts.

"Of course you don't," the Premier says with an edge of a smile. "Always the pragmatist, always making the instant assessment. Are you recording all of this, Joss?"

"Everything," I reply. My fingertips dancing, I am

intent on not missing a nuance of this man and what is occurring in this room.

"Why are you doing so, Joss?" His tone is polite, inquisitive; I sense my answer is consequential to him.

I look in vain for clues in his dark eyes as I reflect over the question. Since he has returned to us our recorders, I have accepted that there must be a reason for his doing so, and like Africa I fail to see it and am suspicious; and I am in fact at a loss as to how to explain or even suppress my compulsion to record as I always do. Perhaps simply to keep my fear at bay? "History," I say. "Large or small, with each life history is made, and I am bearing witness to my own. People die, history perhaps can exist after them for a time."

I don't know who is more surprised—this man, who is looking at me in startled approval, or me, at the warmth and intensity of that approval.

I am bewildered by Theo Zedera's behavior. He appears perfectly sane, everything he says sounds perfectly sane, except that none of it makes sense in any frame of reference, and I see no reason for any of his actions other than that he is a man who enjoys activities like examining butterflies before he goes about tearing their wings off.

"This *is* history, Joss," he tells me, and gestures to the ceiling and walls of the room. "I'm using full-dimensional recordings to preserve every aspect of this moment in history also, but I suspect your version will be the one that has credibility and mine must match up closely with it."

Africa says in exasperation, "*What* moment in history? *What* are you talking about?"

"Africa, finally a question from you."

"Theo, is it a requirement for me to ask before you tell me whatever it is you've placed me here in this cage to tell me?"

He half-smiles. "We have to start somewhere as to my reasons for my...activities since you left. I thought you would at least be curious about—"

"All right. How long have you had the blueprint for your atrocities?"

"From the beginning. But I did miscalculate. All this time I thought I had only to concern myself with keeping this from you and diverting certain requests for assessment away from you. Then it turned out that you were also keeping me in the dark."

More circular talk. Africa just shakes her head. "Very well, Theo, count me as curious. What did I keep you in the dark about?"

"That you planned to disappear."

"How inconvenient for you. What information did you keep from me? In short, what beginning are you talking about?"

"There are many beginnings—"

"Pick one," she suggests acidly.

"There was a beginning three million years ago. There was a beginning two hundred thousand years ago. There was a beginning fifteen thousand years ago."

Africa sighs. "All right. You're referring to human origins on our birth continent of Africa, then the dawn of Homo sapiens, then the presence of the human species on this American continent."

General Desmond looks as confused as I'm sure I do, and Africa speaks for both of us when she asks, "What does the origin of humankind have to do with—"

"Everything," he replies. "It has everything to do with everything. As a synthesist, there was the one area you were never directly involved in—"

"Your area, of course. Sociology, genetics. Why this roundabout—"

"Context, Africa," Theo finishes.

I can so easily see that these two were the closest of friends. They interrupt each other like two partners performing a complicated dance step who know exactly how the other will be moving next.

"Context is vital," he continues. "Sociology was my province, but it was so extensive, so germane to everything you did that it overlapped onto all the information that flowed to you for synthesis. You received an enormity of facts, countless pieces of a puzzle. But sheer volume never stopped you, would never have prevented you from putting every one of those pieces together—had you been given the questions that came to me instead. From the beginning of our careers together I had a suspicion based on what I'd learned of sociology. I made sure you were never given the focused questions that would have allowed you to fit those pieces together until I myself had fit them together."

Now she is intrigued. "Questions. What—"

"Let me lay out the pieces as I saw them. The key ones, the big ones first. War, the biggest one. Murder, rape, assault, every type of violence. What all this violence has in common."

Africa crosses her arms, and does not offer a response, as if this is a philosophical realm too obvious and well-trodden for discussion. But this is central to me. The central issue I grew up with. My worldview that this man personifies. I made a journal entry when we first made Sappho Valley our home, and I remember it exactly: *From age two, when I first learned to read, history told me that this world I found so visually beautiful and so spiritually wondrous, an inspiration for my very early creation of music, is in reality a place of terror. When I look at human history, what stands out? Atrocities.*

Bloody conquests since time began. Leaders of conscripted armies standing on mounds of corpses and thumping their chests in glory.

So I am emboldened to give voice to a response to Theo Zedera's "key pieces" at the risk of angering Africa: "Violence of every type has never ceased. Only increased." The voice of my despair. Undoubtedly not what Africa would say out of her wisdom and brilliance.

Africa flicks a glance of mild reproof at me, then: "True. Simplistically," she concedes in a grudging tone.

He nods at me, and again appears pleased. "More pieces. Nuclear weapons testing—and use. Use of biological weapons and antibiotics. Pesticides. A thinning ozone layer. Greenhouse gasses. The Indo-Chinese biological war combined with release of other varieties of pathogens over the centuries from previous biological warfare."

"Grievous damage to Mother Earth and her atmosphere," I say when Africa again does not offer a response.

"What else?"

I have no answer.

"Still more pieces, then. Longevity drugs and birth control. Alcohol and narcotics. Male erectile-enhancing drugs. Fertility drugs. Artificial food additives and reengineering. Organ transplantation. A life span potential approaching two hundred years. Plummeting birth rates. Cloning. Ovavoid. Estrova."

Africa shrugs. "A mixed bag of positives and negatives. Still not enough information, Theo."

The look he gives her is mournful, as if she is being willfully unforthcoming. Undoubtedly she is. She says, "Whatever your insane game is, Theo, I'm not interested in playing it."

"It's by no means a game, Africa, nor is it even remotely

insane." He turns to his general. "Lucan, would you agree that women's primary function is to have and nurture children, and that men should take care of their families and control and protect the process?"

"Of course, sir. It's the way things were meant to be. And they should always have stayed that way," he adds darkly.

"What do you think of male homosexuals?"

"They disgust me. I tolerate them—I have to, there are so many of them. But they truly disgust me."

"And lesbians?"

He raises his eyebrows, manages a bleak smile since he's in a room with two of them. "At least we have something in common." The standard and oh-so-tiresome cliché. The general, I note, has temporarily ceased checking his communicator and seems absorbed in what is happening in this room.

The Premier says to him, "You would agree that even before the Takeover anti-female rhetoric had risen to unprecedented levels?"

"Yes, sir, but understandable, considering the emasculation that's gone on. And now this Estrova business—it's perverted. It's not the natural way things were meant to be."

Neither Africa nor I respond or even react to this rhetoric, which we've heard all our lives.

Theo Zedera turns to me. "Joss, you're fully aware of the importance of the discovery of Estrova."

Of course I am. He has made a statement, not posed a question. But he awaits my response.

Estrova. I mull over what I will say. In my interpretation of history, I see three momentous events exclusively impacting the destiny of women. The original struggles for emancipation, the pioneers who gave women a first inkling that they could participate in the course of their own lives and in their governance. The second, the discovery of birth control, followed by the side-effect-free Ovavoid in the twenty-first century that—so briefly—set women safely free from being consigned to the fate of brood animals. Both events opposed vehemently, with religious and political fervor and intensity and relentless determination that biology was women's destiny, foreordained and immutable.

Then Estrova. An offshoot of twenty-first-century mapping of the human genome—Dr. Connie Estranza's monumental discovery in 2185 of how to combine the motile ovum from one woman with the sessile ovum from another to create exclusively female life. No greater pitched battle or more fanatical crusade has ever been waged so instantly over a discovery than the one to suppress Estrova, and women stood no chance whatever of prevailing. One week after the introduction of the procedure and the first baby produced from it without the benefit or necessity of sperm, Estrova was banned. Buried under an even greater torrent of religious and medical condemnation and legislative hysteria than what once surrounded abortion. All samples of Dr. Estranza's work were located and incinerated, her research destroyed. Not only was Estrova outlawed, it was placed in the same category of catastrophe as the black plague and biological terrorism, and every step was taken to eradicate all traces of it. And, some say, its discoverer as well. When Dr. Estranza's body was found, along with that of Maria, her child, and the cause of death ruled murder-suicide, no woman on this planet believed it. But Estrova, it seemed, had vanished like a mirage in the desert.

Until Dr. Lucy Kim. The research assistant whom major religions have called the third millennium's personification of Satan. Even though her sin was to enable creation of human life, not destroy it—life genetically indistinguishable from human life existing anywhere in the galaxy. The heroism of Lucy Kim, who reproduced the blueprint for Estrova, is legendary, as is that of the women who disseminated it worldwide in a twenty-second-century version of the midnight ride of Paul Revere. Like the historical witches of Salem, they were hunted down ruthlessly for their heresy; those who lived to see court proceedings—Lucy Kim among them—were given the death penalty, perhaps not burned at the stake like their historical predecessors but suffering an equivalent bath of laser fire, without any of the traditional moral hesitancy over the putting to death of females.

When the first births of Estrova-born babies were discovered, these children were designated the new pariahs, the shunned. But thousands of homosexual men, learning that Estrova children were genetically undifferentiated from any others in the population and that deception might be employed to assimilate them into society, willingly and secretly colluded with the children's mothers to claim them as their own—for the privilege of fatherhood. Until the first countries passed laws requiring proof of a DNA match to a male father for every single child.

Estrova had made it possible for our Unity to self-propagate. These draconian anti-Estrova laws became the impetus that led to our Unity's decision to leave. Estrova had made it all possible: our decision to leave and to form a society without men.

In summation of all this I say to Theo Zedera, "Without doubt, Estrova marks the momentous event in the history of women on Earth. It represents biological independence for all women everywhere, for all time."

"Precisely. The discovery of Estrova seems more than

coincidental—and it couldn't be stopped regardless of all the effort to obliterate it. It was another major piece in the questions I was evaluating. But the final piece, Africa, among all the pieces of information I had, was that you told me about the existence of your Unity."

Africa's head jerks to me. She could not look more appalled by this revelation if she had been stripped bare under the eyes of the entire world. Clearly, clearly, it is her most closely guarded secret.

This ultimate depth of her grief and despair strikes me with the force of a blow. The real impetus behind her fierce dedication to keep our Unity safe is starkly visible. The one-hundred-and-eighty-degree catastrophic turn of this man away from the man she thought she knew had not only been beyond her capability to predict, it was beyond any capacity of hers to change. To risk contacting him would risk exposure of our location. To inform us that she had told him of our existence would have uselessly escalated our fear.

"Knowing about the Unity," Theo Zedera says, "is what made everything I did possible."

I am thunderstruck, but Africa—if a person could will an event to happen, Africa Contrera would will herself to be stretched out lifeless on the floor before me, with a bloody knife from each member of our Unity protruding from her. "What on Earth do you mean?" she whispers to Theo Zedera.

"These are some of the facts you had, Africa." He ticks them off on his fingers: "The birth rate falling. Female births rising to outstrip male births, with the current rate six to one. The number of homosexual men and transgendered male-to-females escalating to thirty-five percent of the population. Male potency in a steady ten percent decline since the twentieth century."

"There are explanations," Africa says in a dead voice. "Including the likelihood of anomaly."

"Women," General Desmond declares. "It's because of the way women turned away from their true roles as wives and mothers. They changed everything from the way it was meant to be."

Ignoring Desmond just as Africa and I do, the Premier gets to his feet to pace in front of our cube. "The worldwide sperm counts and fertility numbers—even allowing for the extreme range of anomaly—were suspicious and significant. The first undeniable confirmation that none of the traditional explanations worked was the Indo-Chinese biological war. It's the first great war with huge casualties that did not produce a population explosion. It meant we were undergoing a sea change in evolution "

"*Evolution*?" I am bewildered. "What kind of evolution?"

"It doesn't matter, Joss," Africa says. She is slowly gathering herself together again, sitting straighter. "It's grotesque fallacy. A Stalinesque use of political philosophy to justify human butchery and the seizing of power. Whatever his sick rationale for committing his atrocities, this claim is fallacy. Yes, population numbers have been dropping for the last two centuries and gender proportions are skewed—these are due to technological advances, increased longevity, persistent pockets of overcrowding. Prior to the mid twentieth century, voluntary population control wasn't a factor for reducing population—birth control was nonexistent. Major medical breakthroughs were yet to happen. Much technology had yet to appear. Life expectancy had made no dramatic advances."

Theo Zedera shakes his head. "You're talking about *after* the great wars, Africa."

"Of course."

"I'm talking about before. *Before* every great war there's been an explosion of the birth rate."

"There has?" This from Desmond. "That doesn't make sense."

"It...actually does." Africa's eyes are suddenly clouded with thought. The rest of her reply comes slowly. "It's true. Before every great war in history our numbers worldwide abruptly, drastically increased out of all historical proportion. The most persuasive theory is a species-level awareness. At the most primitive level of consciousness the human race is like a hive of bees, with a collective awareness, a rudimentary telepathy. So before those wars the human race knew at the species level that catastrophe was coming, we knew we needed to increase our numbers."

"Correct," Theo Zedera says. He is looking at Africa in unblinking intensity, as if she has made a crucial connection.

"But it didn't happen this time?" Desmond asks.

"No," the Premier answers, his eyes fixed on Africa. "This time the decline in birth rate continued before and after the Indo-Chinese war."

"You're right. You're right, Theo," Africa says. Her gaze is distant, as if she is computing a complex array of equations. "I was given no data, no question, and no reason to make this connection..." She focuses on him from where she sits on the floor. "Evolution," she finally says, her voice scarcely audible.

"Precisely." And then Theo Zedera says: "It's the reason I did all of this."

Desmond gapes at him. Africa...Africa tries, but cannot speak. Her legs collapse and are outstretched on the floor, her arms are limp, her head bowed. She looks like a broken doll.

Being a synthesist, she has put all these disparate pieces

together. General Desmond's stare rotates from his commanding officer to Africa to me. Seeing perhaps a kindred spirit, he holds out his hands to me, palms up, in a universal gesture: bewilderment. I make the same gesture back to him.

It is General Desmond who speaks. "Sir, I don't—"

"Lucan," the Premier says, "you're here now because you deserve to receive an explanation. And Joss, you require one."

Mute, I simply nod. Africa is frozen immobile, and my pulse pounds with fear. To comprehend the dark rationale that has led to this day of my probable execution may lessen the fear, may bring me to that same frozen place with Africa. I want to know what this man is talking about. As a mere recorder of these proceedings, I need to know.

"I want to understand." General Desmond speaks for me. "Why wouldn't our collective consciousness work before the Indo-Chinese war?"

"It did work," Theo Zedera says. "That's the point, you see? We tried. How many children do you have, Lucan?"

He stirs in his chair. "Sir, as you know, my career—"

"I've been with countless women and have no children with any of them, never a pregnancy, never a hope." Zed's admission has come with the ease of long acceptance. "How many families do you know with more than one offspring?"

"One...but they used fertility boosters," Desmond concedes.

"So men have diminished potency," I say. "Isn't there still an argument to be made that this is historical balancing, that with our longevity advances Earth remains overpopulated even with a low total of two billion people?"

"I hear it from my troops..." Desmond muses as if he

hasn't heard me. "Most of them use fertility boosters and most of them still can't make a baby..."

Africa says to the Premier in disbelief, "Diminished male potency is the cause behind all this?"

"*Lost* male potency is behind this, Africa. And Estrova. And escalating male violence."

"Taken to its ultimate extreme by you." But the bite has gone out of her voice, and she is looking at him strangely. "What are you telling us, Theo?"

"A sea change in evolution and natural selection has happened. A major biological shift. It's accelerating. What I'm telling you is this: Everyone who's always said that Earth is more than a ball of dirt and rock and water is right. Everyone who's always said that Mother Earth is not a concept but a living entity—Gaia—is right. This is what you told me from the start, Africa, and all this time I believed you absolutely."

General Desmond is shaking his head. "This is *crazy,*" he mutters. "All this time I believed in you, and all this time you were crazy."

The Premier strides over to his general, waits till Desmond meets his stare. "Lucan, listen to me. The evidence is clear. Incontrovertible. We've had an epoch to prove we're a viable dominant species, and we've failed just like the last dominant species on this planet. We're done."

At this pronouncement there is silence in the room. Even one of those silences from the ocean when the tide seems to pause.

Then Desmond leaps to his feet. "You mean the *dinosaurs*? They were wiped out by a *meteor*!"

Surely the Premier will not attempt to change this history. It's established fact that during the Mesozoic era a meteor produced a massive particle cloud that shrouded

Earth and ended the reign of the dinosaurs and all animal life, paving the way for the dawn of humankind.

"True for the dinosaurs and true for us," the Premier says. "We've been wiped out by the meteor we created ourselves. Our own unending violence combined with environmental degradation and chemical reengineering of our bodies. Yes, we're virile, yes, we can have all the sex with all the women we want. But—you have no descendants. I have no descendants. You can pull the trigger on a gun all you want—with no ammunition, nothing happens. Over a period of three million years we've done nothing to evolve. We're done."

"Sir, *sir*," shouts Desmond. He gestures vehemently around him, wild arcs meant to take in much more than the surrounding room with all of its opulent furnishings. "You can't be right. Whatever the numbers say—there's a way to fix this, there has to be. How can women be better than us? We did all this. Men. *Men.* Look at what we did. Everything. We did everything. Women didn't do this. What they did do didn't amount to—they didn't do *anything*. Everything from longevity to space travel—*we* did it. *We* did it!"

The Premier has been listening patiently to all of this. "You're right that we do have more to show for ourselves than the dinosaurs did. A few achievements to leave behind with our fossil bones. Things like the pyramids, some technology, some art—the best of us may remain after us for a time. It's all beside the point, Lucan. What matters is that sociologically we've advanced only a few inches beyond that other failed attempt that Mother Earth dispensed with three hundred thousand years ago, the Neanderthal. What is being selected now is woman."

As Desmond stands there shaking his head at Theo

Zedera, Africa muses, "A failed major life form is hardly unprecedented... Since life on this planet began, natural selection's consigned ninety-nine percent of it to extinction."

I'm shaking my head right along with General Desmond. "You've brought us here to explain that doom is imminent and your slaughter of nations and the enslavement of women are all relevant to...evolution?"

"They are. Thanks to Africa I revere Mother Earth—Gaia—and I'm trying to preserve her."

"*Preserve* her?" I exclaim. "By burning her, by bringing chaos—"

"The laser-burn patches are already healing—coming back as forest where there was desert. And as for chaos—Africa, who was a better witness to chaos than you? We've done nothing but repeat our history of violence, in greater dimension. What difference did you or I or any other advocate for peace ever make, except momentarily? With all our idealistic passion and diplomatic skill—the truth is, we were irrelevant. The violence never stopped—it only grew. Wars—more and more destructive. Everything pointed to the certainty that we'd take everything down with us. I needed to tell you, explain. But you vanished."

She asks, a hand to her throat, "You did all this...because I wasn't here?"

"Of course not. I acted because Lucan joined me and the pieces were in place."

Lucan Desmond makes an inarticulate sound and sinks into his chair.

"Theo—what difference would it have made had I been here? Did you actually expect me to agree with you? Help you? Help with the slaughter of nations? Condone what you did?"

"Never. Women..." He shook his head. "Your survival

depended on stopping what would destroy this world. You couldn't do it. You don't have it in you."

"To do what you did? *No, we don't.* We *don't* have it in us. We never will. What is this? The ultimate playing out of the ultimate male fantasy? You ride in on a white horse to do the unthinkable and unspeakable—kill and kill and kill—to save the women?"

He says softly, "I couldn't save the many of millions of you who died during the Takeover. Many will still die. But many will live. That particular male fantasy appears to be the only course left open. We're the ones who made the weapons, and unless something stops us we'll use them till we destroy everything—and we've proved it. From the time you told me about your Unity I knew you were women who could emerge and heal this world and lead the way to wherever you'll now take it. I had to find you."

She shakes her head. "It was the sheerest accident that you did."

Theo Zedera smiles. "I'd narrowed down where you were. But it was still a race against time. I needed to find you without harming you or before you harmed yourselves. I knew you wouldn't defend the place you've made your home."

"We did defend it," I protest. "We just didn't do it the way you would."

He directs his smile at me, and it seems pitying. "You had no conventional weapons."

"We refuse to call weapons 'conventional.' We don't believe in using your weapons."

"Yes—I know, Joss. Now you'll have your chance to test whether a species of human practicing nonviolence and nonconfrontation can survive."

He turns to General Desmond. "It's finished, Lucan."

"I need...I need to know," Desmond says dully. "About Esten Balin..."

I glance at Africa. Who is Esten Balin? I have no knowledge of who this might be. Neither, clearly, does she.

The Premier contemplates his general. "You told me he was dead, Lucan. Or as good as."

"He is dead, sir. With everything you've said here, why did you keep such a monster near you, so close beside you day after day?"

Theo Zedera nods, as if commending the logic of the question. "To remind me. To remind me day after day why I was doing what I was doing. Why I had to." He gestures toward us. "Release them, Lucan."

The general does not respond. Staring down at the blue carpet, he looks suddenly vacant, depleted, virtually catatonic. After a lengthy, searching gaze at him, Theo Zedera himself dissolves the sides of our cube.

Africa and I come out of our imprisonment, although what it is that we have come into and how it is now to be defined, I do not know. I rub my wrists as though they have been bound.

With no wall between them, Africa Contrera and Theo Zedera stand before each other, this man and this woman. They do not touch. It may be possible for Theo Zedera to do so, but I know it is not possible for Africa. She could not touch this man who has done such deeds. They simply stare into each other's eyes.

She asks quietly, "What from here, Theo?"

But he turns away from her gaze, to address me. "There's something important I need you to do now, Joss." Then he turns back to Africa. "There's much you still don't know."

"Perhaps there's still time... Theo, perhaps if..."

"No," Theo Zedera says in a voice of flat finality. "It's at the species level, Africa. We've always known to protect you—we never truly understood why, not consciously, but we made a religion out of it. We despised anything female and we never questioned why. We hated homosexual men so viscerally that we killed them—and never questioned why. We mated with women and we hated and brutalized you and we never questioned why. But at the species level we've always known why. We've always known you would replace us."

2201.10.05—OLYMPIA

Can this be true? Or is it a ruse?

This is our quandary.

The encampment below Tiptree Forest has packed up its equipment, dissolved its force fields; all the soldiers have boarded their ATVs and departed our valley, clouds of sand and dust rising from the valley floor behind them. The Rule Canyon contingent has just followed.

How to interpret this? There has been no sighting, not a trace of Africa and Joss. We do not know whether they are safe or dead or captured. Our assumption has been that if they had been captured our invaders would remain here to launch a determined search for us, but that is not necessarily correct. They may have withdrawn to simply wait for us to make a move or emit some signal that will enable them to precisely pinpoint and then trap us. At the same time we realize we must act—we have no choice. Our message over the IFC to the ship containing our sisters will eventually be traced to this valley, and if we are to survive we must immediately devise a plan to abandon our home.

Now. Suddenly. Another ATV has entered our valley. A single black-and-gold vehicle emblazoned with the markings of Earth's Premier Supreme. It is landing just below Tiptree Forest in a swirling maelstrom of sand. And immediately has taken off again. Within the enveloping turbulence of the vehicle's departure stands a figure.

Tara is first to make out who it is. "*Joss,*" she gasps.

Joss, knowing that we see her, taps insistently on her wrist pak.

Her first words when we activate her communicator: "Our Unity is safe. Africa is safe."

She is inside our amphitheater, walking directly toward the council platform, looking neither right nor left at any members of the Unity that flank her, arranged in two columns, standing in absolute silence, although some reach to touch her, to reassure themselves that she is not a hologram.

Her expression is impassive. She looks exhausted. What could possibly have transpired? Imagination fails me.

Tara, her slender body almost sagging with release from tension, grasps Joss's hand and speaks first, her voice tear-filled: "Did...they harm you?"

Her reply to Tara is a brief shake of the head.

Isis's first words to her: "Where is Africa?"

I am Olympia the historian, and so when I manage to speak, my first words to her are a historian's open-ended question: "What happened?"

In answer to all these queries, she places her personal recorder on our council table and activates it.

It is now two hours later. We have viewed and heard the events that transpired in the office of Theo Zedera and sit digesting this stunning sequence of events. Joss, after again witnessing what she has just lived through, stares into a sightless distance and seems in a state of paralysis.

"Joss," Isis says gently, and repeats her question: "Where is Africa?"

Joss swallows, then reports to us stolidly: "With Theo Zedera, esteemed Isis." Before we can clamor to ask the obvious, she adds, "This action is her own—freely chosen. It is where she believes she must be."

Foolish woman that I am, this is insufficient for me. "When will she return?" I blurt.

She turns her sapphire eyes on me. In them is a depth of remote ancient wisdom that I hope I will never again see in a woman of such tender years. What has happened to Joss since she went into the desert with Africa—and I suspect we may never learn the full story of that journey—has transformed her irrevocably.

"Esteemed Olympia..."

I take her hands, squeeze them, try to press warmth into them. "Dear one, an answer is not required."

Our Africa is gone from us. Forever.

Tara asks, gently, "Joss, the Interplanetary Frequency Channel..."

"It is clear for our use, Tara," Joss replies quietly.

Moments later, we send in Morse code our "all clear" message that we are safe, and that Earth now awaits the landing of our Unity's visiting craft.

Moments later, the reply arrives: *I knew you girls would manage.*

2202.1.01

Lucan Desmond lounged naked in a beach chair on the shore of the Caribbean Sea, at St. Croix. In the gentle rays of clear, warm sun, naked children, dozens of them, built sand castles or ran and shrieked happily in the calm, turquoise waters. Several dozen women, of all races and ages, also naked, managed to combine talking with one another in the tropical beauty of the day with keeping a watchful eye on their children.

Everything he had ever dreamed of was his. The four palatial houses behind him—his. The town, the entire island—his. Occasionally he idly turned over in his mind whether he would rename the town Lucan and the island Desmond. An island previously named Virgin, renamed Desmond—why not? But then again, why bother? Why lay any claim to an island no one else was remotely interested in owning? The new name, along with everything else, would hardly survive him. It wasn't as if Desmond Island would get on anyone's map. No one was making maps these days, not that he knew of.

He did not know much of anything about anything these days. He could easily find out about the changes underway around the globe—he only needed to ask these women—but he was incurious, he could not be bothered.

The Premier—Desmond still thought of him as the Premier—had last night left the coded message that he was leaving Earth, but he gave neither a destination nor a return date. Desmond could communicate with him for an unspecified period of time via the IFC using a specially assigned priority code. He saw no reason to communicate with the Premier.

Since he had left the compound at Cabo San Lucas that last day, he had received no communication, had heard nothing further from anyone in his officer corps. So far as he knew, all of them were dead. Executions, assassinations, however they were classified, had been carried out in the compound itself while he and the two women, Africa Contrera and Joss, were in the Premier's office. Desmond had found out after the fact from the compound's servants that virtually every single soldier on the premise had been enveloped in multiple layers of laser fire from the scanners, leaving only floating dust molecules behind. The Premier, during the period of time he had been working at his desk before the conversation with the women, had entered innumerable DNA codes into the scanners, and to Desmond's knowledge every soldier in his military in a command position above lieutenant around the entire globe was dead. All of them except him.

That final day he had walked out of a compound eerily emptied of all military presence and with only servants remaining, cowering in corners, frightened, confused, but already looking around at suddenly unprotected riches theirs for the taking.

His command of the military had been nullified, the military itself had been nullified, left impotent. Every cache of weapons had been destroyed, destruct sequences carried out on all major equipment and materiél. When the Premier had occupied himself for that hour before he had begun his conversation with Africa Contrera and the young woman named Joss, he had been busy indeed. The conversation itself had been replayed thousands of times since on vidscreens in every place on the planet where people gathered. A conversation that would be the basis of all history going forward.

He had survived, the last remaining ranking officer in Earth's military, and he had been rewarded for his loyalty.

His loyalty.

Desmond picked up his drink, drained it. One of the women, tall, tanned, and beautiful, with high shapely breasts, pulled herself away from an animated conversation and strolled over to refill it.

He vaguely overheard what they were discussing. Although he sought no news, he could not avoid their continuous, obsessive topic: Ferdinand the Messiah. Women all over the island still talked of it—no amount of discussion seemed to alleviate the need for an endless post-mortem. With the Premier's central information agency abandoned, other news sources had quickly emerged, but even so, Desmond had no idea how they obtained all their news and so quickly; he had given up trying to figure out how women, no matter how isolated they might be, communicated so efficiently from country to country, even island to island.

Reports of what had befallen Ferdinand's followers had been a huge shock wave circling the globe, befitting what was probably humankind's final and greatest calamity. The women continued to give lip service to the possibility that the stories were either exaggerated or erroneous, but Desmond knew they were not and was certain the women instinctively knew it too.

Ferdinand had summoned his followers, had ordered mandatory attendance at designated meeting areas on

2201.10.30. He would appear that evening in person in Rome, he announced, and elsewhere by hologram, to deliver instructions in a momentous message of ultimate atonement, cleansing, and absolution. His followers obeyed. At these gatherings of millions of white-robed males on all the continents, their Messiah appeared in their chanting midst. His arms raised, the black-robed Ferdinand told them the end of the world had arrived, and it was that very day. They would all now die in atonement, to purify the Earth for those coming after them, who would be worthier.

The camps had been surrounded by force fields, imprisoning those within and insulating them from any who would interfere. The followers of Ferdinand the Messiah had ingested the narcotics they had always taken at their mass rallies, and the narcotic taken by these men proved fatal. The few who did not take the narcotic for whatever reason were slain by black-hooded lieutenants especially designated as assassination squads by Ferdinand. The carnage, apparently, was in the hundreds of millions, all of it in the camps within the force fields.

As he picked up his fresh drink, Desmond thought of the woman who was now at the Premier's side. Africa Contrera would have tried to prevent this final Armageddon. She would have been helpless to do so. Outside of Ferdinand and his lieutenants, the end-of-the-world date had been the Premier's exclusive knowledge; not even Desmond had known it. No one knew the whereabouts of the Premier, or Africa Contrera. Possibly in orbit, on the last remaining laser satellite, rumor had it.

Earth systems were running. More or less. Those up and functioning were those chosen by women as necessary. Food production and distribution, child care. Decisions that were theirs to make.

He watched the children at play, watched the tide in its eternal graceful progression. One of the women brought him a plate of fruit, which he accepted with a smile and picked at with little interest. He had children all around him to enjoy, women all around him who were looking after him with casual, indulgent generosity. They could well afford to. They were Femina sapiens. He was irrelevant.

2202.1.01—JOSS

Decision day.

It is late afternoon. I sit on a deserted Pacific Ocean beach at what feels like the geographic end of the Earth. The last time I was here I did not know my location. I am in front of the abandoned compound at Cabo San Lucas where only two short months ago I was witness to the end of world as I knew it. It is here I have come for this private ceremony, not to Sappho Valley. It is here I want to be and need to be, to finalize this decision.

I watch the waves roll in, long green-blue combers, and try to imagine waves of coral, the great coral-colored oceans I have seen in the representations brought to us from Maternas.

When our visitors from Maternas arrived, I did not record the events after the shuttle craft *Lucy Kim* left the *Connie Esperanza* in Earth orbit and landed on our desert landscape. Choked with emotion at our reunion, I felt no compulsion to do anything except view the scene, absorb it into my pores and bones; and so I left it to others to capture the occasion, especially when Mother, our indomitable Mother, first stepped out onto the salt pan below Faderman's View in Sappho Valley, gathering her flapping green lustervel cape around her as best she could in our gusting desert winds.

I look at the scene on my recorder as I sit here—I cannot view it often enough—and again simultaneously smile and cry at the sight of her standing erect, her cantaloupe-size breasts outthrust as she gazes in amazement at several willy willies, our desert dust devils, which are dancing to the side of the *Lucy Kim* as if in mad welcome of her. Then, and only then, does she turn and face us, and her daughters Isis and Olympia at the head of our welcoming party.

Her first words: "Great Geezerak. My dear ones, you didn't exactly pick yourselves a garden spot to call home."

Weeping, yet also grinning foolishly as she seizes the hands Mother holds out to her and then the precious woman herself, Olympia manages to respond, "There were a few limitations placed on us, Mother. We had a problem while you were gone."

"A problem? From what I've heard, from what I've seen from orbit, the planet went to hell in a handbasket."

"It did, Mother, and then some," Isis answers, laughing through her tears as she too embraces her Mother. "We have a lot to report—"

"You'll make your briefing brief, won't you, dear?" Mother says, patting her daughters. "You know how details bore me."

Olympia smiles. "Of course, Mother. Welcome back to Earth."

And with that, with Mother's official welcome having been accomplished, the rest of the passengers, beginning with members of the Inner Circle, disembark from the shuttle craft to further cheers, to screams of greeting and shrieks of delight. From the information and images sent to us when the *Connie Esperanza* broke through the Einsteinian Curve after our all clear signal over the Interplanetary Frequency Channel, I knew that none of my birth family would be on board. The IFC channel has been abuzz with communications, all of us wanting news of this and that loved one, and my birth family has sent me their recorded greetings and news. Even so, this symbolic ending to the cruel partition of our Unity feels exactly like a family reunion and I cry in my joy.

I watch Minerva, our historian here on Earth before she bequeathed the task to her sister, Olympia. She leads the way, with a powerful-looking young woman whom I know to be her lover, Christa, beside her. Followed by Hera the astrophysicist, perhaps the most charmingly arrogant woman I have ever known, who turns so that the wind sails her cape grandly behind her as she stalks out onto the sand to look around in haughty disapproval. Then tiny, sweet little Vesta, gifted psychologist and an even more gifted cook, perhaps the finest in the universe, being helped down by her beloved Carina. And Megan. Who organized the preparations for flight and then led the escape from Earth. Megan, with her remarkable emerald eyes—the same color as Mother's—surveying the horizon line of this, her home planet; blade-slender Megan, in her white shirt and black pants and high boots, striding to Olympia and Isis and their enthusiastic embrace, and then to the tearful greeting of her sister Tara, and then the rest of us in the Sisterhood.

More of our sisters spill out of the *Lucy Kim* before it takes off to bring down the rest of our visitors. I regret that of all those who have made the journey, Venus is not among them—the reason being, from the whispers I've heard, that she was too preoccupied with her latest dalliance. The legendary and scandalous amatory adventures of this particular member of the Inner Circle have always entertained me, but now they seem inspirational. She makes me realize that I have eighty years before I reach her century in age, and I can only hope that my vigor will match hers.

I remember it was at that moment, as I stood among

our welcoming party, that I noted everyone from Maternas looked older. Discernably older than when they had left…

"I'm proud of you, my dear ones," Mother addresses all of us, her contingent here on Earth. "I'm proud of all my offspring but I'm especially proud of all of you. Now that we're free to go back and forth, some of you will surely come back with us. We've all been lonely for one another."

A simple request with large complications: a long trip, and a time warp. It is now three years and four months since the rest of the Unity left Earth. But when Mother and her contingent left Maternas to return here, the equivalent of twenty-five years had elapsed there. They journeyed through a time warp coming back—to discover that a mere one-eighth of that time had elapsed here. So any visitor from Earth to Maternas will discover that she is considerably younger than those who had previously left Earth. I would be much younger than my formerly younger sister, Trella... This time warp phenomenon, Hera has informed us, should be a one-time event. She has every confidence that another route can be plotted through the star systems, around the time warp…and perhaps the entire confusing paradox can be corrected. *Perhaps*. A large word, in this context…

In these intervening two months since their arrival, Earth has been much changed. It has staggered under the shocking blow of the incomprehensible carnage instigated by Ferdinand the Messiah, a devastation to the ranks of men that beggars imagination or description. Even though several hundred million remain alive who were not a part of the cult of Ferdinand, they pass their days in states of acute depression and narcosis. What has happened, physically and psychologically, can only be described by Theo Zedera's analogy of the meteor that wiped the dinosaurs from existence. Even Mars Base has been affected, seceding from its obligations as an Earth military base, classifying what has happened on

Earth as a contagion that has affected them as well.

Even though Mother Earth is beginning the long, slow emergence from the nightmare of destruction visited upon her by Homo sapiens, much is happening neither voluntarily nor easily. The major armaments accumulated by nations were destroyed during the first hours of Zed's Takeover, but caches of weapons, some substantial, were still hidden here and there throughout the globe during his rule. They have now been ferreted out and destroyed by satellite-directed laser blasts. No one knows for certain how their locales were determined, but the best surmise is that it has been the work of a gifted synthesist putting together satellite patterns of troop and militia movements from decades past. Next, all DNA scanners were destroyed by precision satellite-directed laser fire, ending all further possibility of using individual DNA codes ever again as weapons. And finally, one of history's spectacular meteor showers was produced four weeks ago when a laser satellite destroyed all of its neighboring satellite weapons in their orbits, the debris raining through the atmosphere of a surprised world in a spectacular golden shower that dissipated before it reached the surface.

Which still left small arms, and according to news reports these continue to be found in copious quantities and men continue to loose them on one another at the slightest provocation. Many surviving males have tenaciously held onto these weapons, secreting them, often threatening their use if confronted with a demand to relinquish them. When the women in a locale learn of the existence of such weapons, they approach these recalcitrant men in one of two ways, depending on behavior analysis. If the men are irrational for chemically induced reasons, which is often the case these days, a band of women use tranquilizer drug darts of the sort used to bring down an injured animal so that it can be treated and released. They then remove and destroy the weapons from these tranquilized men. If the owners seem rational—as rational as anyone can be who wishes to retain weapons—then a group of several hundred of us gather and simply walk toward the weapons with hands outstretched until they are either turned over to us or the men are engulfed and the weapons gently taken from them, to be dissolved in an acid bath. A few of us were injured this way before men ceased their firing on unarmed women; thus far none of us has been killed.

Conditions continue to slowly improve, especially since our focus has been on food gathering and shelter, not on armament or enforced control over others' lives. The oddest, most ironic happening: After all my unhappiness over having to live in Sappho Valley, it has become a pilgrimage for women from all over the world. Enchanted by our underground realm, they flock to the view into Bannon Crater, into our decorated rock rooms, through our mural-covered tunnels, into our hydroponics chambers, and most especially into Tiptree Forest. Our valley has become a prototype for other designs incorporating Mother Earth herself as shelter. Our gay brothers have joined with us, have come safely out of hiding to place their considerable gifts into the work of protecting and preserving this newly configured world.

As for myself...because of my role in the meeting between Theo Zedera and Africa, I am far too visible for anything close to comfort. I am recognized everywhere. Attendance overflowed at my one music concert—not for my music, I realized, but because of my presence in the events involving Africa and Theo Zedera. I do not wish to make music here again.

No less a personage than the leader of our expedition to the stars, Megan herself, has met with Tara and me, asking us to return with her to Maternas, where our talents would be put to good and needed use. Tara remains undecided, and seems troubled that I received this personal request from Megan—a great compliment and opportunity. It would be good to go to a world where I can be assimilated without fanfare and be myself again, and where I can rejoin my birth mother, Silke, and my sister, Trella. And I would have a purpose there—to assist with a problem with Maternas's young women, a problem that intrigues me because of its mystery: Megan will give no specifics other than that her daughters Emerald and Crystal are involved...

I will go.

The paramount goal of my life has been fulfilled—my reason for remaining on Earth. Africa...

That day four months ago, after the recorders had been turned off in the office of Theo Zedera in the compound just behind me, after he had informed me that General Desmond would return me to Sappho Valley to report to the Unity what had occurred here, she took my hands and looked into my eyes and simply said, "I believe you know what I must do."

I looked into her eyes and said within the depths of me, *I love you. I will love you forever.*

I could not say it aloud. I could not place another burden upon her. And so I said to her: "I understand that you must remain with him."

And she kissed my forehead. And said, "Joss..."

It is beyond my powers to describe how she said that word.

Theo Zedera said to me, simply: "Go forward."

Then they left me. And that is the last I saw of her.

And so I have needed to come here, to this place where I last saw her, was last with her, to make my solitary farewell.

No one else knows where they are now; the current

guess is that they occupy the one remaining satellite in orbit. No one knows the truth but me.

In a personal message over my communicator she has told me this, and asked that I not repeat her message because Earth, while some men still exist, is better served for now by the possibility that Theo Zedera has potential to act against them.

Last night the two of them disarmed the one remaining satellite, and they have expelled themselves from it in its shuttle pod.

Such a pod is designed for orbital repairs, not survival in space. When its propulsive thrust has concluded, one of the planets will pull it into its gravity and to extinction, or perhaps they may fall into the sun.

I think of them seated side by side, waiting, knowing precisely when their ship will reach its incandescent end, because she is a synthesist and will have computed it. I think of Theo Zedera accepting this final destiny as he has accepted all of his destiny, this man who learned from history that he must set a sequence of events into motion, this man who learned from Africa Contrera how he must do it. I picture Africa reading the data of the transformation of Earth while it can still reach her. I picture her gazing out at the planets and stars all around her, haunted to the last by what has been done and awaiting the welcome release of her death.

I will go to Maternas. But they are within me always, these two who have ushered in a new epoch for humankind.

This man named Theo. This woman named Africa.

Acknowledgments

To Jo Hercus and my indispensable inner circle: Monserrat Fontes; Clarice Gillis; Cath Walker, Ph.D.; Paula L. Woods. Many, many thanks to all of you for the careful readings and invaluable feedback. An additional note of gratitude to Cath Walker for the wonderfully informative biology information.

To Angela Brown, my editor, not only for lifting my own work but for her strong presence at Alyson.

To the entire Alyson team. I am proud to have my work under the imprint of the publishing company that has served the entire LGBT community so long and so well.

To a number of research sources that provided crucial information: *Annals of the Former World* by John McPhee, Farrar, Straus and Giroux, NYC, 2000; *Death Valley: Geology, Ecology, Archaeology* by Charles B. Hunt, University of California Press, Berkeley, CA, 1975; *Geology Underfoot in Death Valley and Owens Valley* by Allen F. Glazner and Robert P. Sharp, Mountain Press Publishing Company, Missoula, MT, 1997; *Volcanoes: Crucibles of Change* by Richard V. Fisher, Grant Heiken, and Jeffrey B. Hulen, Princeton University Press, Princeton, NJ, 1998; *Introduction to the Physics of Rocks* by Yves Guéguen and Victor Palciauskas, Princeton University Press, Princeton, NJ, 1994.